# *Wopper*

## HOW BABE RUTH LOST HIS FATHER AND WON THE 1918 WORLD SERIES AGAINST THE CUBS

### *Volume 1*

# *Pigtown*

#### YOUNG ADULT VERSION

NEW HANOVER COUNTY
PUBLIC LIBRARY
201 CHESTNUT STREET
WILMINGTON, NC 28401

## By Frank Amoroso

simply francis publishing company
North Carolina

Copyright © 2017 by Frank Amoroso. All Rights Reserved.
Young Adult version

No part of this publication may be reproduced, stored in a retrieval system or transmitted, in any form or by any means – electronic, mechanical, photocopying, recording or otherwise – without prior written permission from the publisher, except for the inclusion of brief quotations in a review.

All brand, product and place names used in this book that are trademarks, service marks, registered trademarks, or trade names are the exclusive intellectual property of their respective holders and are mentioned here as a matter of fair and nominative use. To avoid confusion, simply francis publishing company publishes books solely and is not affiliated with the holder of any mark mentioned in this book.

Library of Congress Control Number: 2017900274
ISBN: 978-1-63062-011-0 (paperback)
ISBN: 978-1-63062-012-7 (e-book)

**Publisher's Cataloging-in-Publication**
*(Provided by Quality Books, Inc.)*

Amoroso, Frank L., author.
  Wopper : how Babe Ruth lost his father and won the
1918 World Series against the Cubs / by Frank Amoroso.
  volumes cm
  Includes bibliographical references.
  CONTENTS: Volume 1. Pigtown -- Volume 2. The Show -- Volume 3. The Series.
  ISBN 978-1630620097 (volume 1)

  1. Ruth, Babe, 1895-1948--Fiction. 2. Ruth, Babe, 1895-1948--Childhood and youth--Fiction. 3. Ruth, Babe, 1895-1948--Friends and associates--Fiction. 4. World Series (Baseball)--(1918)--Fiction. 5. Baseball players --United States--Fiction. 6. World War, 1914-1918--Evacuation of civilians--United States--Fiction.
7. World War, 1914-1918--German Americans--Fiction.
8. Biographical fiction. 9. Historical fiction.
I. Title.

PS3601.M668W67 2017        813'.6
        QBI16-900097

For information about this title or to order other books and/or electronic media, contact the publisher:

simply francis publishing company
P.O. Box 329, Wrightsville Beach, NC 28480
www.simplyfrancispublishing.com
simplyfrancispublishing@gmail.com

Although every precaution has been taken to verify the accuracy of the information contained herein, no responsibility is assumed for any errors or omissions, and no liability is assumed for damages that may result from the use of this information.

The views expressed in this book are those of the author and do not necessarily reflect the views of the publisher.

Every effort has been made to determine and acknowledge copyrights, but in some cases copyrights could not be traced. The publisher apologizes for any such failures and upon written notification will remedy this in any subsequent editions.

## OTHER BOOKS WRITTEN BY FRANK AMOROSO

### *Behind Every Great Fortune®*

". . . boldly imaginative historical novel that is sumptuously detailed and filled with intrigue, betrayal and plot twists that surprise and entertain the reader."

### *Dread the Fed*

". . . a gripping story of a crime so bold, so ingenious and so perfect, that a century later, the plunder continues and the People venerate the banksters who commit it."

### *Behind Every Great Recipe*
### *From Latkes to Vodkas & Beets to Meats*

". . . a charming and unique companion book containing delicious period recipes and vignettes featuring the characters from the historical novel *Behind Every Great Fortune®*."

Louis J. Amoroso, catcher, St. John's University (circa 1939)

# Dedication

To my father Lou who embodied all the noble qualities of fatherhood. He loved, protected, provided, taught, inspired, supported and comforted us when we faltered. My mother, brother, sister and I were blessed to have Dad as the rock of our family.

Among his greatest gifts to me was the gift of baseball which has brought me so much joy! My Dad was a catcher who taught me so much about baseball and engendered my love of the game. *Wopper* explores the father figures (real & imagined) in the life of Babe Ruth, the greatest ballplayer who ever lived.

I'm reminded of the brothers who loved baseball and made a pact that the first one to die would return and tell the survivor whether there was baseball in Heaven. After the first brother died, he appeared in a dream to his brother and said, "I have good news and bad news. The good news is that there is baseball in Heaven. All of our old buddies who died before us are here, too. Better than that, we're all young again. Better still, it's always spring, and it never rains or snows. The fields are perfectly manicured; there are no holes or bad bounces. We can play baseball all we want. Best of all, we never get tired."

"That's wonderful," said the other brother. "It's beyond my wildest imagination! So, what is the bad news?"

"The bad news is that we are playing a doubleheader this afternoon and you are pitching the second game!"

My hope is that my father will be my catcher when I pitch the second game.

Author with Dad at Ferry Point Park, Bronx, NY (circa 1957)

# Foreword

Babe Ruth is the greatest baseball player who ever lived. Period.

Babe revolutionized the way the game was played and he saved the game from the stain of the Black Sox scandal. His accomplishments were so phenomenal that a new word was added to the language in his honor. The word "Ruthian" is an adjective that means: "Of a prodigious accomplishment" and as applied to baseball means "Prodigiously accomplished with respect to batting, typically describing the flight of a long home run."

The name Babe Ruth is synonymous with the highest standard of excellence. For example, the great Italian tenor, Enrico Caruso was called the Babe Ruth of opera singers. George Bernard Shaw was called the Babe Ruth of playwrights. And Willie Sutton was known as the Babe Ruth of bank robbers.

# WOPPER VOLUME 1 PIGTOWN

Baseball is a sport driven by numbers. Fans of the game take great pride in spouting stats to support any contention that can be imagined especially when comparing players from different eras. The variety of statistical measurements that have been applied to measure baseball performance is truly a marvel of modern computers and the Sabremetrics, popularized in the book *Moneyball*. By any measure, Babe Ruth stands as a titan above anyone who has ever played the game.

When Babe Ruth retired from baseball he had set the record in 54 major league statistical categories. The one he cherished most was the consecutive scoreless innings pitched in the World Series that lasted for 44 years. Pitching mostly for the Red Sox, (he was 5-0 as a Yankee) Ruth had a lifetime record of 94-46 and an ERA of 2.28. There is no question that he was one of the premier pitchers of his generation and probably would have gone to the Hall of Fame as a pitcher. His talent for blasting home runs gave him baseball immortality.

His most famous records were his single season home run record of 60 that lasted for 37 years and the most career homers of 714 that lasted for 53 years. He set and broke the single season home run record four times. To provide some context on Babe's home run prowess, he hit more home runs than any other team in the American League in two different seasons (1920 & 1927). Not only was Ruth incredibly productive, he was reliable. During his

# FOREWORD

Yankee career, Babe played in 2,083 games out of a possible 2,310. Babe Ruth's superiority relative to his peers is legendary. More books have been written about Babe Ruth than any other American sports figure.

So, why another book about Babe Ruth?

Babe Ruth was a natural showman with a flair for the dramatic. He was also an outsized personality who was prone, perhaps, to excess. These characteristics have been repeated so often that the image of Ruth in the popular culture is a cartoon character – a clown of a man who regularly ate a dozen hot dogs, drank half a dozen beers, chased women, and blasted home runs for a sick boy in a hospital to lift his spirits.

The image of a bloated Babe in his mid-thirties is one that prevails in the popular perception. Through his twenties and early thirties Babe Ruth was a trim, explosive athlete, standing around 6' 2" and weighing about 195 pounds. He was a gifted baseball player who stole home plate ten times during his career. Throughout this book there are pictures of a lean, rangy Babe Ruth to make the point that he was a true athlete.

None of the books written about Babe Ruth explore in depth his relationship with his father and other men in his life. I learned that Babe's father was killed in a street fight outside his saloon in Baltimore just nine days before the 1918 World Series. At the time, Babe was 23 years old and was scheduled to start game one of the World Series against the Chicago Cubs. Apart from an occasional mention of his father's death, there is virtually nothing written about the emotions that the young son must have experienced. Nothing about the grief, the anger, or the regret has been chronicled. This series attempts to remedy that deficiency.

In my series *Wopper – How Babe Ruth Lost His Father and Won the 1918 World Series Against the Cubs*, I portray a Ruth who experiences the heartbreak of his first love, the pain of family tragedies, and the anguish of making the right choices and the sorrow when loved ones die.

Another aspect of life that sports books often leave underdeveloped is the historical context that may have profound influence on the participants. In 1918, the United States was embroiled in the First World War. As a country with many German immigrants, America was deeply divided. The 1918 World Series opened in Chicago amid a tumult caused by a mortal struggle between super-patriotic American groups and pro-Kaiser German groups. The day before the World Series was scheduled to begin, unknown persons detonated a bomb in a federal building in the middle of Chicago, killing and injuring dozens. Months earlier, a German alien had been lynched outside of Chicago. Furthermore, the Department of War had declared that baseball was nonessential and ordered the players to "work or fight" after the season ended. These intense events most certainly would have impacted members of the Red Sox and Cubs. Yet, not much has been written about the impact of these events on the ballplayers.

# FOREWORD

*Wopper: How Babe Ruth Lost His Father and Won the 1918 World Series Against the Cubs* is my attempt to fill these voids.

I have divided the story into three books because each presents an important aspect of the whole that warrants independent development. Volume 1, **Pigtown**, is about his early childhood days in Baltimore and the influences on the young Jidgie through his fabled days with Brother Matthias at St. Mary's Industrial School. Volume 2, **The Show**, details Babe's professional baseball career and stormy love life during his rocky journey to major league stardom. *Volume 3,* **The Series**, recounts the turbulent and violent events of 1918 that culminate with explosive force during the World Series.

The word **Wopper** in the title is a whimsical variant of the word *wap* which means to strike forcibly, or in its noun form the sound of something being struck forcibly, or, alternatively, a tall tale.

Each may be read separately as a stand-alone, or, collectively as a real wopper!

Given that more than a century has obscured the early life of America's greatest baseball player, the best way to communicate the story is to novelize his early years. I have used the vernacular of the day in a way to provide authenticity without distracting. A glossary of early 20th century slang and idioms is included in the back for the reader's convenience. For example, fans were known as cranks or bugs and team owners were known as magnates.

**Wopper** attempts to lift the shroud of Babe's early life using the drama of story-telling and the tools of historical fiction. Some relationships, conversations, and timing have been created or connected to enhance the impact of the story. None of these negate the essence of the drama surrounding the humble beginnings and early career of George Herman Ruth, Jr. The goal of any imagination, speculation, or conjecture in this novel is to entertain, titillate, and provoke the reader.

Before entering the labyrinth of our protagonist's life, the reader should know that prior to writing this book, I received a literary license to imagine, speculate, and create scenarios that may or may not have occurred, but that are within the realm of possibility. Most of the events depicted actually occurred; however, there may have been some modifications for dramatic effect. Many of the characters are real persons. Some of the characters are fictitious; others are used fictitiously. When the actual words of an historical figure appear, they are denoted with internal quotation marks and referenced in endnotes.

As was aptly stated by Mark Twain:

Persons attempting to find a motive in this narrative will be prosecuted; persons attempting to find a moral in it will be banished; persons attempting to find a plot in it will be shot. BY ORDER OF THE AUTHOR.

Enjoy *Pigtown*, Volume 1 of
*Wopper:*
*How Babe Ruth Lost His Father and Won the 1918 World Series Against the Cubs*

Frank Amoroso
Wilmington, North Carolina

# Ruth Family Tree

## Paternal Grandparents

John Anton Ruth (1844 – 1897) Babe's paternal grandfather.

Mary E. (Strodtman) Ruth (1845 – 1894) Babe's paternal grandmother. Both were born in Maryland of German heritage. John's parents were born in Prussia, and Mary's parents were born in Hanover.

## Maternal Grandparents

Pius Schamberger (1833 – 1904) Babe's maternal grandfather.

Johanna Schamberger (1836 – 1900) Babe's maternal grandmother. Both maternal grandparents were born in Baden, Germany.

## Babe Ruth's Parents

George Herman Ruth, Sr. (1871 – 1918) Babe Ruth's father

Katherine "Katie" Schamberger Ruth (1873 – 1912) Babe Ruth's mother. She lost 6 of 8 children and two brothers.

### Children

George Herman "Babe" Ruth (1895 – 1948)

Augustus Ruth (1898 – 1899) who was born on March 15, 1898, but died at the age of 1 year and 1 day.

Mary Margaret "Mamie" Ruth (August 1900 – 1992) Babe's sister. "See, there were many children in our family, but they were all deceased, other than Babe and I. Babe was the firstborn. I'm the fifth. There was a sister to me, a twin. Twin girls and a set of twin boys. But Babe and me were the only ones to survive."

William Ruth (1905 – 1906) Babe Ruth's youngest brother who died when he was one.

## Babe Ruth's Wives

Helen Woodford Ruth (1896 – 1929) Babe's first wife who died mysteriously in a house fire.

Claire Hodgson Ruth (1897 – 1976) Babe's second wife.

## Babe Ruth's Children

Dorothy Helen Ruth (1921 – 1989) adopted by Babe Ruth when he married Claire Hodgson.

Julia Hodgson Ruth (1916 –    ) Claire Hodgson's natural born daughter from her first marriage. Julia was adopted by Babe Ruth when he married Claire Hodgson.

Julia, Babe & Dorothy Ruth

# People, Places and Things

**Dante Aquaviva (1884 – 1967)** childhood friend of Kate Schamberger Ruth and one of the Three Musketeers with Pasquale Gaetano and Jidgie Ruth.

**Leo Bilski (1884 – 1971)** irascible right-handed pitcher who was banned from major league baseball for headhunting.

**Brother Matthias Boutilier, C.F.X. (1872 – 1944)** the prefect of discipline at St. Mary's Industrial School. By all accounts he was a huge man; some say he was 6'5"and 300 pounds. Known as the Boss, Matthias famously tutored Babe in the finer points of baseball, especially, power-hitting.

**Bunny Hole Gang** – band of rapscallions led by Babe Ruth consisting of Jidgie, Stash, Little Jake, Bullet, Knobby, Barefoot, Runt, Gunny and Noodles.

**Enrico Caruso (1873 – 1921)** world's greatest opera singer in early 20th Century and lead tenor for the Metropolitan Opera.

**Soldano Cefalo (1892 – 1957)** cousin of Colina Petronilla and protégée of Enrico Caruso.

**Walt Disney (1901 – 1966)** substitute letter carrier in Chicago before becoming the founder of the Disney entertainment empire.

**John Dunn (1872 – 1928)** successful manager and magnate of the Baltimore Orioles in the International League who signed Babe Ruth from the schoolyard of St. Mary's Industrial School.

**Frank "Tug" Figaro (1887 – 1973)** catcher for the Ottos for the game at Old Bethpage against Frazee's Crazees.

**Mick Flanagan (1879 – 1951)** former major league catcher whose career was interrupted by domestic obligations. He went to work as a prison guard with the New York State Department of Corrections at Sing Sing where he developed a reputation as a mean-spirited sadist.

**Harry Frazee (1880 – 1929)** theatre impresario who purchased the Boston Red Sox in 1915 and notoriously sold Babe Ruth's contract to the New York Yankees before the 1920 season. Many baseball fans believe that this transaction spawned the 'Curse of the Bambino' that prevented the Red Sox from winning the World Series until the curse was broken in 2004.

**Pasquale Gaetano (1888 – 1973)** friend of Dante Aquaviva and member of the Three Musketeers along with Jidgie Ruth.

**Oscar Gnarltz (1884 – 1961)** manager of the Baltimore Terrapins in the Federal League, major league infielder, third base coacher for the 1918 Chicago Cubs.

**Henry Nicholas "Gunny" Gunther** (1895 – 1918) contemporary of Babe Ruth and native of Baltimore who earned distinction while serving in the U.S. Army during WWI.

**Jolly Brothers Club** – fraternal society for German-Americans located in Baltimore, Maryland. George Herman Ruth, Sr. was a member.

**Otto Hermann Kahn** (1867 – 1934) famous financier, raconteur and philanthropist who inspired the creation of the iconic symbol of the board game Monopoly®. He was the chairman of the Metropolitan Opera and neighbor of Colonel Jacob Ruppert, owner of the New York Yankees.

**Louis "Fats" Leisman** (1896 – 19??) friend and classmate of Babe Ruth at St. Mary's Industrial School for Orphans, Delinquent, Incorrigible and Wayward Boys. Fats published a monograph in 1956 about life at St. Mary's during the time Babe lived there.

**Fritz "Flash" Maisel** (1889 – 1967) buddy of Jack Dunn, magnate of the Baltimore Orioles. Led the American League with 74 steals for the New York Yankees in 1914. His manager, Frank Chance, called him "the cleverest base runner in the league."

**Oinky** a Yorkshire crossbreed of the type of pig herded from B&O trains down Ostend Street to slaughterhouses in South Baltimore. She was rescued by Babe Ruth.

**Brett "B.O." Oakwood (1886 – 1960)** legendary major league pitcher whose career ended prematurely due to his self-destructive abuse of alcohol.

**Colina Petronilla (1896 – 1954)** New York native and contemporary of Babe Ruth who spent her summers in Baltimore and became a member of the Bunny Hole Gang.

**Pigtown** Baltimore neighborhood that acquired its name from the herding of pigs through the neighborhood from the railyards to the slaughterhouses.

**Gavrilo Princip (1894 – 1918)** Serbian nationalist whose assassination of Archduke Franz Ferdinand in Sarajevo on June 28, 1914 sparked the outbreak of WWI.

**Colonel Jacob Ruppert (1867 – 1939)** an American brewer, businessman, National Guard colonel, and United States Congressman who purchased the New York Yankees in 1915.

**St. Mary's Industrial School for Orphans, Delinquent, Incorrigible and Wayward Boys** a school operated by the Brothers of the Order of St. Francis Xavier that was located several miles outside the city of Baltimore, Md. In the early 20th century it was a residential facility that housed approximately 800 students who were a combination of delinquents, orphans and those who paid tuition. When Babe Ruth entered St. Mary's in 1902, Brother Dominic was the headmaster at St. Mary's.

Statue of young Babe Ruth outside Oriole Park
(author photo)

# List of Images*

- vi   Louis J. Amoroso, catcher, St. John's University (circa 1939)
- vii   Author with Dad at Ferry Point Park, Bronx, NY (circa 1957)
- viii   Frank Amoroso
- xv   Julia, Babe & Dorothy Ruth
- xx   Statue of young Babe Ruth outside Oriole Park
- xxii   The Pigtown section of Baltimore, early 20th Century
- 4   Cropped picture of infant Babe Ruth with mother Katherine (circa 1895)

    Babe Ruth as a toddler

- 16   George Herman Ruth, Sr. with wife Katherine Schamberger Ruth
- 28   Oinky

    Early picture of extended Ruth family and neighbors

- 40   St. Mary's Industrial School early 20th Century

    Brother Matthias and Babe Ruth

- 50   Baltimore, Maryland early 20th Century street scene (circa 1906)
- 72   Enrico Caruso
- 113   Colina Petronilla (circa 1917)
- 114   Mary Margaret "Mamie" Ruth (circa 1920s)

    Babe Ruth as a teenager at St. Mary's

- 141   Signature of George H. Ruth
- 145   *Wopper Volume 2 The Show*
- 146   St. Mary's Industrial School Baseball Team. Babe Ruth back row center (circa 1913)

*The poor quality of some of the images provided was unavoidable due to limited availability of early pictures of Babe Ruth and his environs.

# *Wopper*

HOW BABE RUTH LOST HIS FATHER AND WON THE 1918 WORLD SERIES AGAINST THE CUBS

## *Volume 1*

# *Pigtown*

YOUNG ADULT VERSION

The Pigtown section of Baltimore, early 20th Century
(courtesy of the Babe Ruth Birthplace Museum)

# Opening

"Hey, kid, I like that dress. Something about the colors reminds me of the flowers that bordered the path to our casita when we was in Cuba. You know, ours was right next door to Rico's. We would sit on the veranda smoking our stogies and listening to the serenade of the tree frogs. '*Bambino*, he would say, if only . . .' and he would puff his cigar like this."

The man pumped air until his cheeks expanded like a tree frog's throat sack. His dark brown eyes twinkled. He winked to his daughter and exhaled, blubbering his lips. They shared a laugh until the nun at the nurse's station brought a bony white finger to her lips and shushed them. The effort of stifling the laugh brought on a coughing fit.

"Oh, Dad," she said, lifting a glass of water toward him, "Take a sip. It's time for your pills."

She was her father's daughter with the same kind face that always brought comparisons to the moon. Dorothy glanced at the clipboard hanging from the foot of her father's bed. The black metal bars of the footboard made her think of a cage and how his gentle spirit was caged in his deteriorating body. He was only fifty-three years old; yet, the cancer in his throat has robbed his vitality, his robustness. Looking at his skeletal form covered limply by the hospital sheets, her eyes welled up.

# OPENING

In her mind's eye, she is eight years old. The sun is shining brightly. The standing room only crowd presses against her; but, somehow, she finds the closeness comforting. Her feet crunch peanut shells that seem embedded in the Stadium floor with a gluey mixture of spilled beer and soda. The noise is so loud that her brain can only focus on the man standing adjacent to a white rubber plate with a beveled edge. It is home plate at Yankee Stadium, 1927: the epicenter of the baseball world.

It is the last game of the regular season and the score is tied in the home eighth. There is a runner on first base. The men around her are wagering as to whether or not he could do it. Do what? She thought.

"I bet you a beer that the big fella won't do it," said the thin man whose mustache and pointy nose reminded her of a fox.

"Ya don't know a thing about baseball. Of course, he'll do it. He's already hit sixteen this month," said the man with the stub of a cigar protruding from his fleshy lips.

"This is his last at bat of the season, it's dark and he's facing a lefty. There's no way," said fox-man.

"Ya think Babe's afraid of that lefty Zachary? Ha, he's already gotten two hits and a walk off him," said cigar-man.

"That's exactly why Zach is gonna get him this time; he's due. That's the way baseball works," laughed fox-man.

"OK, Mr. Baseball, you're on," said cigar-man.

She pictures her father standing in the batter's box, waggling his bat slowly in the way a cat's tail sways as it stalks its prey. He is using the reddish bat he calls Bella. All the cranks are standing, screaming for all they are worth.

Sixty feet, six inches away, a man nervously paws at the dirt in front of the rubber slab and fingers a baseball, searching for the proper seam to impart enough spin on the ball to create movement that will avoid the sweet spot on the bat. At least that's the theory, he tells himself and he winds up to deliver the rock in this primal battle against the man with the stick.

As the spheroid approaches her father, he cocks his bat and unleashes a mighty swing that whooshes toward the ball. Hardwood collides with horsehide, yarn and cork, and produces a thunderous crack. Instantaneously, the ball flattens then trampolines off the bat with a velocity that propels it into a rainbow arc that defies gravity. The crowd inhales almost as one.

The ball is soaring. But wait; it's hooking toward the foul pole. No one in the park is breathing. Like a comet traversing the heavens near a planet, the white spheroid is close to the pole but it passes a mere six inches to the inside. Fair ball!

The crowd emits a deafening roar when the baseball lands. Her heart races as she visualizes him mincing around the bases with his unique pigeon-toed stride. Third base coacher Charley O throws his hat skyward and he provides a royal escort to Babe as he trots down the last line to home. Homer number sixty, unbelievable.

His eyes are closed. The incessant pain in his throat fades as the sedative kicks in; he is floating weightless, pain free. He glides inside a familiar building, clad with limestone and encircling an emerald green ballfield. Floating along a concrete concourse he approaches an opening and enters a large, open rotunda. There, a line of people shuffles forward. At the head of the line is a girl. Dark-haired with hazel eyes, she points to a woman. She is thin to the point of emaciation. Tears roll down her gaunt cheeks.

Great sadness overtakes him as he hovers over these two people. He is falling. The two faces are disembodied. They swirl around him asking, pleading for something that he cannot provide. He is falling.

Cropped picture of infant Babe Ruth with mother Katherine (circa 1895)

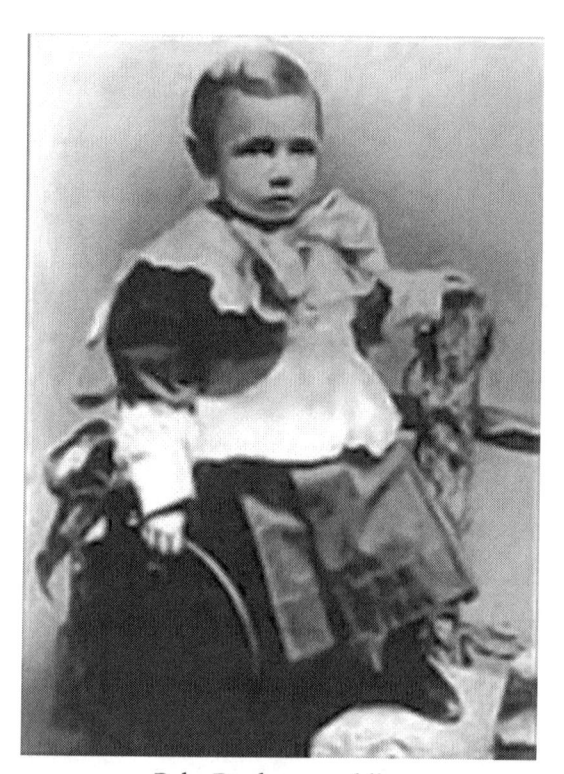

Babe Ruth as a toddler
(courtesy of the Babe Ruth Birthplace Museum)

# 1

# 1902
# Baltimore, Maryland

> "Who knows, he may grow up to be President someday, unless they hang him first!"
> ~ Mark Twain

"Stop 'em, stop 'em," shrieked Mr. Braun to no one in particular. "When I get *mein* hands on you, I'll wring your little necks!"

The stout man wore a blood-stained butcher's apron and waved a glistening cleaver as he chased the culprits. Lagging further behind with each step, the exasperated shopkeeper lapsed to his native German to curse the boys who responded with laughs and taunts. With the veins on his neck protruding like the over-stuffed *bratwurst* the boys had pilfered from his shop, the butcher stuttered to a halt. Gasping for breath, he bent over his ample belly. Muttering German curses under his breath, he watched as the boys weaved through the traffic and disappeared out of sight.

"Hey, Jidgie, slow down, we lost him," said Gunny between gulps of the cool winter air.

"Yeah, wait up," pleaded Stash. "I got a stitch in me side." He clutched his side and stopped running. Bent over like the handle of a water pump, he watched the dark-haired boy disappear into the crowd ahead at Camden Station.

"Come on, Stash," rasped Gunny, his breath still coming in gulps. "Jidgie won't stop 'til he gits to the Bunny Hole."

The boys walked together for several blocks until they entered Pig Alley, the dark, stinky alley that ran between Dover and Camden Streets in the Pigtown section of southwest Baltimore. As they approached a row of gritty wooden barrels along the side of a brick wall, the boys slid behind the last barrel through a ragged chink in the brick wall emerging in the crawl space under a vacant warehouse. With mock reverence, their sanctuary was named after the Black Rabbit, a shabby tenement house located several blocks away at the northwest corner of Camden and Eutaw streets, where Noodles and Stash lived.

The Bunny Hole was the headquarters of the Bunny Hole Gang. The gang consisted of nine boys under the age of ten. They were the children of German, Czech, and Hungarian immigrants who worked in and around the stockyards, breweries, and docks of Baltimore. Jidgie was their unofficial leader. He was the fastest, strongest, and most impulsive when it came to daring fun. It also helped that he supplied the boys with an endless supply of tobacco, root beer, and French postcards that he filched from tipsy patrons of his father's saloon. Jidgie loved a good time and the boys knew that he loved sharing everything he had.

Their leader had discovered the Bunny Hole quite by accident. One afternoon when Jidgie ran into Pig Alley to escape an irate shopkeeper, he wedged himself behind some old barrels. Several bricks in the wall came loose. Unable to find the hidden boy, the frustrated baker departed, admonishing that he would tan his hide when he found him. Jidgie pushed and wiggled at the bricks until he opened a hole large enough to crawl through.

He found himself in an enclosure studded with beams and posts. It had a dirt floor and a ceiling riddled with rusted nails from the flooring above. It was the perfect hideout for Jidgie's band of rapscallions.

Over time, the boys had dragged in all sorts of flotsam and jetsam to make the space, in Jidgie's words, "jest like home." The dirt floor was soon covered with a ring rug that Gunny had pilfered from a clothesline on South Eutaw. Light came from nubs of candles that Stash had taken from St. Hildegund's where he was an altar boy. The smell of the melting candle wax helped mask the musty smell of their headquarters.

Scattered around the rug were a couple of wooden boxes and an old, ratty mattress that Noodles found in the railyards discarded from a caboose. Their prized possession was an old carriage seat that Jidgie had found by the docks and dragged to the sanctuary. They covered the errant springs with a prickly old horse blanket that Mr. Holzmacher, the blacksmith, had discarded last June. Eventually, the ripe, horsey smell dissipated and the carriage seat became the symbol of leadership for the band of miscreants.

Jidgie was ensconced on the seat when they arrived. At his feet was a circle of cobblestones containing a dented, copper cuspidor filled with charcoals that were glowing red under a crust of gray ash. Grimy, metal skewers filled with the stolen brats were draped across the wide rim of the makeshift grill. The brats sizzled and smoked, filling the confined space with a mouthwatering aroma. Jidgie prodded a few potatoes that were embedded in the coals.

"My fellow Bunnies, you done good. Thanks to the slow butcher, we will be chowing down on these tasty brats and taters shortly. And, I have a special treat for the gang," he said with a mischievous glint in his eyes.

He was tall for a seven year old. His thick, curly, black hair outlined a round, moon-shaped face. It was hard to describe his features because his face was a kaleidoscope of laughs, smiles, smirks and winks. On the rare occasions he was not in constant motion, his dark eyes revealed a bright intelligence and infectious joviality. Despite his prodigious appetite, he was whippet-thin.

His Christian name was George, after his father. His nickname came from the mispronunciation of Georgie by his younger sister. When his father first heard baby Mamie speak the name Jidgie, he guffawed and declared it his son's nickname. The name stuck until he became a professional baseball player many years later.

"Hey, Jidgie, I found this bar behind Holzmacher's and thought we might be able to use it," said Stash, presenting a twisted angle iron.

"What good is that?" scoffed Gunny. "The bloody thing is bent. Why don't you take it back to the blacksmith and ask him to straighten it?"

The group laughed derisively. Jidgie watched as Stash slumped his shoulders and lowered his eyes. Jidgie took the bar from Stash and, with a concerted grunt, pulled it straight.

"Wow!" murmured several of the boys.

Jidgie emitted his high-pitched laugh and said, "Let's eat. I'm starving!"

The gang gathered around and speared at the brats with sticks. When each of the boys had a steaming brat and potato, Jidgie pulled out his surprise from beneath the carriage seat. It was a blue growler of root beer, compliments of Ruth's Saloon, located on West Camden Street. It was owned by Jidgie's parents, George and Kate. The Ruth family lived above the tavern.

He put the rim to his lips, paused, winked and took a long deep swallow. The boys passed the growler around as if it were a golden chalice from the tabernacle at St. Hildegund's.

When the tasty meal was done, Jidgie removed the stub of a cigar from the top pocket of his overalls. Striking a match on the coarse fabric of his butt, he lit the cigar. A loud belch erupted from deep within his belly. Sated, he settled back into his throne.

"Hey, Stash, put some wood on the fire. We need more light," ordered Gunny.

The growler made its rounds as the boys settled into a contented stupor. The boys took turns telling wild tales of adventures that they would have in the future.

⚾ ⚾ ⚾

A short distance away, at the corner of West Camden and South Paca Streets, another George was holding court in a saloon he owned in Pigtown. The neighborhood was a mishmash of meat packing and cold storage warehouses, interspersed with small two-story brick row houses, and Mom and Pop retail stores. The distinctive name came from pigs that were regularly driven through the neighborhood from the Union Stockyards to nearby slaughterhouses after being off-loaded at the B & O rail yards.

The sound of the work whistles signaled the end of the work day. Soon, the evening rush of workmen stopping in for a quick belt before heading home would begin. Then, the dinner crowd would follow.

"Katie, how's the stew coming? Don't forget to put the shepherd's pies in the oven. Did Sullivan deliver the fish?" said George Herman Ruth, Sr., in German to his wife. They were the

# 1902 BALTIMORE, MARYLAND

children of German immigrants and often lapsed into German while working under pressure of operating the family-owned tavern. George had married Katherine Schamberger when they were barely in their twenties. Now, in 1902, they had two surviving children, George, Jr., seven, and the baby, Mary Margaret who was two years old. George, Jr., had nicknamed the baby Mamie because he thought her given name had too many *sylerrbles*. During their marriage, the Ruths would lose six children. Katie was frail and often too exhausted to work in the saloon's kitchen. Throughout their marriage, they struggled, living hand-to-mouth.

After trying his hand as a lightning rod salesman and a street car operator, George became the counterman at a local saloon. Blessed with a gregarious nature, George was a natural bartender. He thrived and soon became the proprietor of the saloon on the main drag in Pigtown.

"George, I can't keep up. Where is that son of yours? I need help with the potatoes," said Katie, also in German, her voice barely audible above the screech of the streetcar brakes as it slowed to round the corner. Baby Mamie sat at the high prep table, tied to a barstool. Her face wore the remnants of her greasy dinner.

"I'm sorry, Katie. I can't leave the bar, the *menschen* from the first shift are coming in and I'm setting up the back bar. When Jidgie gets back here, I'm going to give him what for!"

"Hey, George, don't make us wait all night. We're powerful thirsty," said Willy Schlict, the foreman of the Armour Packing Company.

"Bring a couple of pitchers over to the pool table. Me and the guys are gonna play some eight ball."

"Coming right up, Willy," said George.

"Hey, George, have you seen my growler? I must have left it behind last night. You know, the blue porcelain one," said Hans Klemmer, a stockman over at Swift & Company.

"No, ain't seen it," said George, as he navigated through the growing crowd carrying two frothy pitchers and five mugs over to Willy.

"Darn, my old lady is going to be hacked off. She just bought it for me last Christmas."

"Hans, maybe if you wasn't so sloshed last night, you would have taken it with you when you left," said Billy Tickner, the son of the neighborhood undertaker.

Slapping a barstool, Billy said, "Set your butt down over here. I got the next one."

Hans grinned and ambled over.

"Hey, George, do you know what one undertaker said to the other? Pass me another cold one! Get it?" said Billy. There were a few groans at the joke that the undertaker told every night.

George smiled, thinking that he was attracting a solid core of regulars. He knew that they could get cold beer anywhere, what he needed was good food to keep them coming back. Where was that blasted kid? Katie is working herself to a frazzle and he's out gallivanting with his pals. He'd better show up quick, there's a mountain of potatoes and onions to peel.

George was returning to his post behind the bar when he saw Jidgie trying to wedge behind Gussie Schmidt and sneak along the wall to the kitchen without being caught. Jidgie was almost home free, but he stopped to hang a growler on a peg by the billiards table.

"Stop right there, you little punk," said George Sr. With

astonishing speed for his bulk, George was on his son. The boy stood with an attitude of resignation, like a monkey caught with his hand in the cookie jar. He knew better than to make excuses; he knew what was next. The boy stared up at his towering father, his face contorted with rage. In the boy's attempt to escape, he bumped into the wall, dislodging the growler. It clattered and spun as it hit the floor.

There are different types of silence. The one where the room goes quiet just as someone blurts out something inappropriate is pretty bad. But, the silence that comes when there is a collective realization of guilt is worse. Jidgie faced that silence now as the growler settled flat. All eyes turned toward the youngster with accusing looks. George's saucer-like face, already red with anger, grew crimson when he grasped the situation. His dark eyes turned beady and his barrel chest inflated.

"Is that Hans' growler? Did you take Hans' growler? You are in for it now! I'm going to give you the whipping of your life," said George, unbuckling his belt. There was a tension so thick that it could choke one of the twelve-foot long manatees that lived in the harbor. It enveloped the bar.

Bile rose in Jidgie's throat as he cringed before his angry father. The lower he sank the more the smell of stale beer and sawdust assaulted his wide nostrils. His father folded the thick strap in half and brought his hands together. The leather strap bulged, and then, cracked when his father jerked his hands apart. Jidgie recoiled at the sharp noise, then, gave his father a look that was at the same time smiling, yet, grim and melancholy.

The strap unfurled as George raised it over his head. Hans bolted forward and grabbed the strap from George's hand.

"Now, Georgie, you don't want to do that," said Hans. A

broad grin spread across his face. George was startled. He glared at Hans and then lurched toward him, pushing him hard in the chest. He pushed again and again until both were outside. The saloon door rattled to a stop against the building.

Meanwhile, inside, Jidgie took refuge in the kitchen, but not before he filched a plug of tobacco from the undertaker who had rushed toward the front window to watch the altercation.

"I'll paste you in the bean," screamed George. "No one is going to tell me what to do with my kid." This invective came out in German. Even if Hans had not been fluent, George's intent was unmistakable.

With fists raised, knees flexed, George adopted a fighter's stance. Hans was about to do likewise when he spied a copper rushing toward them. Palms up, he nodded to George. It took a second to register, then, George turned to see Officer Mulroy cruising through the evening traffic toward them.

"Is there a problem here, laddies?" said Mulroy, with a mixture of false sweetness and sarcasm. A beefy hand on his nightstick communicated all that was necessary.

"We're just getting some fresh air, right, Georgie?" said Hans, with the demeanor of a choirboy.

Taking his cue, George draped his arm on Hans' shoulder and unleashed a toothy smile. Another street brawl averted, Mulroy tipped his cap with the knob of his nightstick. The policeman moseyed over to the window and peered into the saloon.

"Mr. Ruth," Mulroy said with mock formality. "Tell me that if I enter your fine establishment that I will not find a minor playing pool the way I did the last time I was here. I would not want to give you another citation."

"No, you most certainly will not. No need for any more citations," said George.

Mulroy smiled.

⚾ ⚾ ⚾

The next day, Jidgie was out of the apartment above the saloon before his father awoke. He walked over to the Black Rabbit tenement to gather up some Bunnies and plan their next adventure. As soon as he turned the corner, Gunny, Stash and Noodles lit up because they knew that the prospects for the weekend just got brighter.

"Come on, boys, let's go over to the train yards and see what came in overnight," said Jidgie.

"Sounds good to me," said Stash.

"Yeah," said Gunny. "Maybe we can find something to pinch."

They walked along the tracks, trying to see who could balance the longest on the rails. That contest lasted until a B & O freight train came barreling down the tracks, with the engineer blaring its steam trumpet at full volume. The boys jumped aside and held their ears as the train thundered toward Camden Yards. Jidgie went to the tracks and put his ear on the rails.

"There's another one right behind her. Watch this," he said. He reached into his pocket and produced a penny. Looking both ways, he bent to place the coin on the shiny, silver track. A minute later, the ground rumbled. The train whipped past them, blowing cinders and particles at them in a rush of air. When it was out of sight, Jidgie raced to the tracks and found an elongated sliver of copper which was all that remained of the penny.

When they got closer to the rail yards, they crept along the embankment to avoid detection by the guards. Once, last year, Gunny had tripped while trying to escape and was caught by the guards, who gave him heck and dragged him to his mother's shop. She was so angry that Gunny was confined to his room for a week. He said that the worst part of the week was missing the adventures of the Bunnies.

As they walked toward the railyards, Jidgie grabbed a few rocks; the others did the same. He took aim at a utility pole that was about twenty-five feet away and let fly with one of the rocks. He hit the pole dead center. There was a wooden thud. When the other boys heaved rocks at the target, there was only the sound of stones clattering harmlessly beyond the pole. Jidgie fired more rocks and each hit the pole squarely. None of the boys came close to hitting the pole, except for Gunny. With both eyes squeezed shut, one of Gunny's throws managed to nick the pole. Soon, frustration set in and the boys abandoned the game, conceding victory to Jidgie.

They continued toward the rail yards and Jidgie withdrew a plug of tobacco and offered a bite to the boys. He took a big chunk and chewed furiously until a bulge the size of a cue ball swelled on the side of his jaw. The chaw seemed like a moon protruding from his already round face. Almost immediately, he squirted a stream of tobacco juice through his front teeth.

"How did you learn to do that?" asked Gunny who struggled to break down the hard plug in his mouth.

"From me Pappy. I learnt from watching me Pappy. Just like I learnt to drink root beer, play pool and cuss. I just copy whatever he does."

"Did he teach you how to throw rocks?" asked Stash.

"Naw, he don't teach me nothing. Can't be bothered. But, I'm a good copy-cat," said Jidgie with a wistful smile.

George Herman Ruth, Sr. with wife Katherine Schamberger Ruth (undated) (courtesy of the Babe Ruth Birthplace Museum)

# June 13, 1902
# Baltimore, Maryland

*"Being a role model is the most powerful form of educating . . . too often fathers neglect it because they get so caught up in making a living they forget to make a life."* [i]
~ John Wooden

George left the saloon after the lunch rush. With Katie and the baby napping upstairs, he had a couple of hours to run some errands before he had to be back to prepare for the evening shift. He was at his wit's end; Jidgie was driving him crazy. The local shopkeepers, the truant officer and, now, the police were complaining about Jidgie's antics. His son's behavior had long since passed being excused as cute, or mischievous. It was borderline criminal. The worst part about it was George's realization that he had no control over the boy. George wanted to understand the boy, but lacked the time and temperament.

His first stop was the Jacob Ruppert Brewery which was just down the block. His mood brightened as he breathed deeply, inhaling the pungent, citrusy aroma of hops that emanated from the brewery. He would not live to see the impact that Jacob Ruppert's son would have on his own son's life.

## JUNE 13, 1902 BALTIMORE, MARYLAND

After placing his weekly beer order at Ruppert's, George headed to the Jolly Brothers, a social club and singing society that celebrated German culture.

"Hey, George, long time, no see," said Fritz, a burly bartender with a baritone voice. He led the club's male chorus.

"We still have a spot for you in our singing group. The German-American National Alliance is sponsoring several competitive singing festivals this summer. We are planning on entering at least three. You should come; it'll be fun."

"I would love to . . . maybe next year. Getting the saloon off the ground requires enormous energy. What with all the cooking and cleaning, Katie is in the verge of collapse. I just can't spare the time."

Fritz slid a dish across the bar. It contained a hefty, beef sandwich slathered with horseradish and mustard on a Kaiser roll. George took an appreciative bite and washed it down with a cool, dark beer.

"What about your kid? He should be old enough to help out by now."

"*Já,* he's old enough, that little *rotz nase*. That one will be the death of me! He just turned seven and already he has more bad habits than me. He smokes, he cusses, he steals. The shopkeepers along Pratt and Lombard are always accusing him and his gang of hoodlums of pinching food. The worst is that he laughs at me when I try to teach him the right way."

"Sheesh, sounds like a handful," said Fritz. "How's he in school?"

"When he is there, he does okay. He likes the German lessons, so he can speak to his aunts and uncles. Jidgie is pretty good at math. When I let him handle the till he does a good job. But, he refuses to read. The gist of the problem is that all he wants to do is *blau machen,* play hookie. He goes to school only when the weather is bad. The rest of the time, he's out gallivanting. I have the blasted truant officer, in my saloon every other day. The only way to keep the truant officer from going to the police is to let him practice on the pool table. That man can certainly play a lot of pool," said George, pushing away his sandwich in disgust.

"It may be none of my business, but if it was my kid, I'd send him to that there industrial school to learn a trade. Those brothers know how to tame them wild bronks," piped up one of the regulars at the far end of the bar.

"Yeah," added Morey. "My cousin had a kid that was incorrigible. They sent him to St. Mary's and those brothers whipped him into shape. The kid now makes a fortune as an entertainer. You know, Moshe Yoelson's boy, Asa. He uses a stage name to hide that he's Jewish."

"You mean that Al Jolson singer? That kid is funny as hell and he can really belt out a tune. I took the missus to see him at the Majestic. We had a grand time," said Fritz.

"George, you should go talk to Brother Dominic at St. Mary's. He'll give you straight answers," said Morey.

"Maybe I'll do that. I gotta run. They drove a herd of pigs past the saloon to the slaughterhouse today. My little *rotz nase* disappeared early in the morning, so, now, I've got to clean up the hog crap in front of the place before the evening rush. It never ends."

"That's why they call it Pigtown," said Fritz, laughing derisively.

Several blocks away at the Bunny Hole, Jidgie was facing a crisis of his own.

It was the custom of the Bunny Hole Gang to assemble in the Bunny Hole after school let out; at least, the ones who attended school. Jidgie preferred to spend his days prowling the neighborhood and the docks looking for opportunities for mayhem. That way, when the gang showed up, he could entice them with his plans for adventure that he had conjured up during the day. On this particular early spring day, he would face a challenge that would

## JUNE 13, 1902 BALTIMORE, MARYLAND

have reverberating consequences.

Usually, as long as he evaded the truant officer who had begun to stake out the Ruth residence early in the morning, Jidgie was free to follow his whims. The truant officer was new on the job. His name was Joe Manker. He was raised in a strict German household where it was a cardinal offense to defy the dictates of the father. Of moderate height and build, he was zealous, conscientious and determined. The school superintendent who hired him thought that he just might be young and determined enough to rein in the ring leader of a group of high-spirited boys before they escalated from petty vandalism to lives of crime. He had seen the pattern before and the end was not pretty.

T.O. Manker was wiry and athletic; traits that were deemed essential to catching the Ruth boy. Previous truant officers had been older, retirees from the postal or customs services, who were adequate at investigating the whereabouts of absent children, but ill-equipped to chase a spry, young buck like Jidgie. After accepting more than a few resignations from exasperated officers, the superintendent decided to try a new approach by hiring the young Manker.

Despite surprising his quarry on a few early morning stakeouts, Manker soon realized that he could not outsmart, outrun or out-hide his target. The Ruth boy was more agile, resourceful, and devious than any seven year old who ever lived. The frustrated Manker soon found himself in Ruth's Saloon each afternoon commiserating with Jidgie's father. The men swapped stories of Jidgie's more outrageous stunts and pondered ways to reform the boy. None of their ideas worked.

⚾ ⚾ ⚾

Meanwhile, Jidgie was not without problems of his own. In recent months, his leadership of the Bunnies had been challenged by Gunny. He was about the same age and, although they were the same height, he outweighed Jidgie by fifteen pounds. With a barrel-chested frame like his father who was a brew meister at Ruppert's Brewery, Gunny chafed at the natural leadership of Jidgie. The stouter boy figured that today was the day he would capture the allegiance of the Bunnies.

Now, Jidgie was on the throne in the Bunny Hole when the Bunnies arrived after school. His rendition of the plans for mayhem that he had devised for the week was interrupted by a commotion near the entrance. Gunny entered the Bunny Hole dragging a burlap sack by a rope tied around the end. The sack bulged and wriggled. Whatever was inside the sack made a shrill sound of pain and terror.

"Hey, Gunny, what ya got there?" said Noodles.

The boys crowded around Gunny craning to see the source of the commotion. Milking the attention, Gunny scuffled to a barrel and sat with the squirming sack on his lap.

"Come on, show us what it is," pleaded several of the boys.

"I will, but first you've got to build up the fire real high," said Gunny, shooing at them.

Jidgie watched with apparent disinterest as the boys scurried around dragging scraps of wood and other flotsam to add to the fire. When Gunny withdrew a pocket knife and opened the blade there was a gasp of admiration from the boys.

"Wow, Gunny," said Stash, "where did you get that?"

"I got it from me Pappy," said Gunny, brandishing the knife over the sack. He cut the rope, pushed it inside the bag and made several jerky motions inside the bag. Bunnies pressed closer. Even Jidgie rose to see what was happening.

With a flourish worthy of a vaudeville magician, Gunny yanked upward. At the end of the rope was a piglet. It was pink and squealing for all she was worth. The boys laughed nervously at the squirming creature. Gunny grinned at the group.

## JUNE 13, 1902 BALTIMORE, MARYLAND

"I snagged her this morning when the herd came through Pigtown."

"How did you do that?" questioned Little Jake.

"I rigged a trap from me basement window. I tied this rope in a noose and laid it on the ground. When the herd stampeded down the street, I yanked on the rope and caught this little bugger."

"What are you gonna do with her?" said Stash.

"Can we keep her as a mascot?" asked Noodles.

"We can call her Oinky," said Stash.

"Nah, we gotta kill her," said Gunny. "Me Bunnies, this here critter is going to make some fine eating,"

A hush settled over the boys as the implication of this statement sunk in. Several of the younger Bunnies drifted toward the perimeter. Gunny sensed a shift in the collective mood. He reached for his knife and opened the blade with his teeth. Standing in the flickering firelight holding the rope with the dangling piglet in one hand and the knife in the other, Gunny presented a primal tableau.

In the corner, Stash cowered with his hands over his eyes. Through his fingers, as he viewed the figure of Gunny in shadow, the knife lengthened and the terrified pig loomed large against the wall. Stash's whimpers were smothered by the incessant squealing of the piglet.

"Ain't gonna be no killing here," said Jidgie.

"Sez who?"

Jidgie pointed to his chest and, then, gestured to Gunny with both hands, a clear invitation. With a ferocity that startled some of the onlookers, Gunny threw the knife into the ground and tied the rope holding the pig around it. He recognized his opportunity to become the leader. Rage filled his eyes. The Bunnies backed away, forming a circle around the combatants. The boys faced off, feinting and mimicking fighters they had seen on the streets. Gunny was hunched over, his breath shallow and rapid. Jidgie stood upright, his dukes held high to protect his face. They shuffled warily.

Suddenly, Gunny roared and charged. As the distance between them closed, Jidgie shifted to the right and pushed Gunny on the back. His momentum was so great that he flew off balance into the dust. The group gasped when they saw that Gunny's lip was split. He spit blood. Gunny scooped a handful of dirt and pebbles and threw it at Jidgie whose left hand blocked it reflexively. Before he knew it, Gunny was on him, fists flailing. One blow caught Jidgie on the side of the head as he moved away. He fell. Gunny jumped on top of him and straddled Jidgie.

In a quick movement, Jidgie shifted onto his opponent's leg and rolled. Gunny toppled over. In an instant Jidgie jumped to his feet. While Gunny staggered upright, Jidgie glided behind him. With speed and power, Jidgie grabbed his opponent from behind, pinioning his arms. Jidgie squeezed with all his might and lifted the other boy off the ground. Gunny struggled furiously, but the bear hug held until he could no longer breathe.

"I give, I give," huffed Gunny. "Stop. You win. Do what you want with that stupid pig. She's yours."

Later that night, Jidgie braided the rope into a harness and proudly led the piglet through the neighborhood towards home. When he arrived, he snuck into the shed behind the saloon and piled up some straw in the corner and tied Oinky to a cornerpost. The animal squealed plaintively when Jidgie left the enclosure. He returned a few minutes later with some leftover cornbread and a bowl of water.

Over the next few weeks, Jidgie cared for the piglet. He enjoyed Oinky's intelligent and affectionate nature. The animal invariably greeted him with unbridled joy, wriggling and squealing whenever her young master appeared. Later in life, Jidgie would remark that

## JUNE 13, 1902 BALTIMORE, MARYLAND

Oinky was his best friend growing up.

The living arrangement worked for a while. Jidgie avoided his father's suspicion by diligently taking the trash out of the saloon to the shed before he was asked. For his part, George thought that his son's new found responsibility was the result of the fear of God imparted by the father's threats. For her part, his mother viewed it as the answer to her prayers. This domestic tranquility would soon be shattered.

Rat-tat-tat-tat. The hailstones pummeled the tin roof of the shed housing Oinky. She squeezed under the damp straw. The sparse hair on her hackles was standing on end. She shivered and moaned in fear and discomfort. A round faced surveyed the backyard from an apartment window in the rear of the building. Jidgie's features were etched in worry. A heavy rain pockmarked the deepening puddles. Jidgie imagined water rising in the shed. He looked at his sister Mamie across the room and wondered how she could sleep through this storm.

Suddenly, a bright flash erupted before his eyes, blotting out the scene. A thunderous crash followed, propelling him out of bed. A terrified shriek outside told him that he had to act now. I can't leave Oinky down in the shed to drown, he thought. Again, more lightning and thunder produced terrified squeals of panic in the shed below his window.

Sprinting down the stairs and past the kitchen, Jidgie grabbed a towel and raced barefoot into the yard. When he threw open the shed door, another clap of thunder struck. As he untied the leash, Oinky leaped into his arms. He wrapped her in the towel and pulled her to his chest. Ankle deep in clammy mud, he hurried back into the house. As quietly as possible he slithered up the stairs, oblivious to the trail of mud in his wake. So far so good, he thought at the landing. On tiptoes he made it into his room. Oinky stopped shivering and remained quiet despite more claps of thunder receding into the night along with the worst of the storm.

Covering Oinky with the towel, Jidgie placed her under his bed. His hand dangled over the side onto her back, providing reassuring caresses. To the sound of rain streaming on the window, he fell into a deep sleep.

Katie barely stirred when Big George arose to start another long day in the struggling tavern. His habit was to brew a pot of coffee before preparing breakfast for the family, while Katie dressed and cleaned Mamie and got his vagabond son ready for school. It had been a restless, stormy night and she lingered in bed for a few extra minutes. Rather than the familiar smell of coffee, Katie smelled something far more disagreeable. Was that rank, barnyard smell coming from inside the house?

"Oh, *mien Gott*! Oh, my God, what have you done!" screamed his mother.

She was standing over Mamie's bed, a look of horror and disgust splayed across her pale face. Katie flashed back to the infant deaths of her babies which she vaguely attributed to life in Pigtown. Jidgie silently arose and stood yawning beside her. Her back heaved with sobs. There, in Mamie's bed, limbs intertwined, lay his sister and Oinky. The mother watched as the filthy pig nuzzled her precious daughter. Katie was beside herself with fear and rage. At the sound of her mother's wailing, Mamie blinked herself awake. As she focused on the animal beside her, she screamed. Katie swooped down and lifted Mamie into her arms. Oinky emitted a sleepy grunt. When she opened her eyes, the pig assessed the situation and did what any other pig would do under the circumstances. She panicked.

Jidgie and Big George chased her through the apartment, up and down the stairs. Their intentions were quite the opposite. Big George wielded a large cleaver and a murderous look. Jidgie bore the fervor of a rescuing angel in his attempt to keep Oinky away from his enraged father. Although Oinky was not greased, she may as well have been. She darted and sprinted around like crazy, knocking furniture this way and that. Finally, Jidgie reached the back door and threw it open just as his father was about to corner the pig. Oinky seized the opening and flew out the door. Jidgie gave a somber wave goodbye to his friend and turned to face his out-of-breath father who in desperation heaved the cleaver at the fleeing pig.

Jidgie stood transfixed, his hands drawn to his broad cheeks, his eyes alight with horror as the cleaver spun end over end toward Oinky. Big George's aim was true and the instrument of death whirred ominously through the air. Run, Oinky, run screamed Jidgie silently, his mind flooded with fear. Suddenly, Oinky's front legs plunged into a muddy rut. Her front end dipped and her butt end rose. Instead of cleaving her skull, the missile caught her tail. Jidgie saw a spurt of blood as the cleaver clattered into the street. Oinky shrieked, but her legs churned faster as she regained her balance and disappeared around the corner.

Jidgie raced after her to no avail. He sloshed through the muddy puddles to retrieve the cleaver. Through blurred vision, he saw Oinky's blood diffusing in the murky water. When he saw the tip of her tail still wriggling, he bent over and retched.

Jidgie barely had time to straighten up when his father caught him by his collar and dragged him back to the saloon, muttering to himself in German all the way.

That night Jidgie lay in bed. After the pig had escaped, Big George had brought Jidgie to his room and nailed the window shut and locked the door along with the admonition that he should reflect upon his actions that caused so much distress to the family.

Later Big George complained to his wife, "The boy is incorrigible, Katie. If we don't knock it out of him now, who knows what sort of monster he might turn into when he gets older."

Later, Jidgie's heart ached from losing Oinky and from the total loneliness he felt in his own home. Only dear, little Mamie gave him any solace. She whispered that she thought that Oinky was cute.

JUNE 13, 1902 BALTIMORE, MARYLAND

Oinky

Early picture of extended Ruth family and neighbors, Babe and his mother encircled on left, George, Sr., front row center wearing bow tie (circa 1895) (courtesy of the Babe Ruth Birthplace Museum)

# June 13, 1902

# Baltimore, Maryland

"It was at St. Mary's that I met and learned to love the greatest man I've ever known. His name was Brother Matthias. He was the father I needed. He taught me to read and write – and he taught me the difference between right and wrong."

~ Babe Ruth

Jidgie had a spring in his step. It was Friday and he and the Bunnies would have the entire weekend to themselves without the annoyance of school. As far as he was concerned school interfered with adventure; that's why he avoided it as much as possible. Right now he approached the local grammar school to gather up with the boys for a game of baseball. He had parlayed three dozen eggs and a sack of potatoes for a scuffed wood bat and a real baseball. His trading partner was a carpenter who played on one of the local company teams that traveled around the city playing exhibition games on the weekends. Even the cool, overcast weather could not dampen Jidgie's ardor. He imagined himself zinging the pill past an overmatched Gunny to secure the victory. A broad smile creased his face.

## JUNE 13, 1902 BALTIMORE, MARYLAND

He was slouching against a wall in an alley across the street from the school when the release bell rang. While scanning the school children for his Bunnies, he dropped his guard. Jidgie realized that he had fouled up when he saw a look on Stash's face. The youngest Bunny, with his eyes widened like a startled cow, pointed at the danger behind Jidgie. He immediately went into evasion mode. Ducking under truant officer Manker's outstretched hands, Jidgie dodged right and wheeled left toward the train station. Unfortunately for Jidgie, Manker had an accomplice who grabbed Jidgie by the collar with one hand and his belt with the other hand. Jidgie's legs bicycled helplessly in the air. The Bunnies who had been flocking toward him, now turned away hiding smirks at the ridiculous spectacle of their leader being carried with limbs flailing.

"Where do you think you are going, son?"

Jidgie slumped in defeat, as he recognized the voice of his namesake. He knew that he could never escape from the barrel-chested man who loomed over him. At that moment Jidgie considered his father to be the strongest giant on the planet. A lost emptiness filled the boy.

Less than an hour later, Jidgie was bathed and dressed in his Sunday best. His father dropped a pillowcase toward him. What's that the boy's eyes questioned.

"It's all yer clothes. You'll be needing them where you are going," said Big George brusquely. "Kate, I'll be waiting outside by the trolley stop."

His teary-eyed mother yanked a comb through his hair. She whispered, "It breaks my heart when I look at you."

Big George's hand firmly grasped Jidgie's collar as they boarded the Wilkens Avenue trolley. Jidgie figured that they were heading to exile at the house of one of his relatives. The backs of his legs pressed uncomfortably against the hard wicker seat. The car jerked forward. The connecting pole on the roof of the trolley crackled and sparked as the trolley navigated from West Camden Street onto South Paca Street. When the trolley crossed the intersecting tracks, the boy nearly bounced off his seat.

Big George sat rigid, staring straight ahead as they passed the stop for his grandparents' house. Although Jidgie had frequently crossed his father, he had never felt such a thick, ice barrier separating them. He fidgeted, looking in every direction trying to discern where they were headed.

Eventually, his father rose at their destination. A chastened Jidgie had never felt so helpless as he dragged his pillowcase in the dust of his father's footsteps. The invisible fetters of paternal discipline encumbered Jidgie more than any chains could. They walked along a pathway that led to the largest building Jidgie had ever seen. The entrance was shrouded in shadow as they approached the massive wooden doors. Jidgie shrunk into his thin cotton jacket. Crossing the entrance foyer, their footfalls echoed loudly, adding further to the boy's apprehension.

"How may I help you?" asked the receptionist from behind an imposing oaken barrier.

"I have an appointment with Brother Dominic . . . concerning my son," said Big George, nodding dismissively toward Jidgie.

"The boy can stay on the bench over there. I'll bring you in to see the superintendent."

While waiting on the hard bench, Jidgie was confused and totally out of his element. All he knew was that he was alone in a strange place and that his father was in an office talking to a super somebody. On top of that he had not eaten since the morning. Suddenly, his belly started churning. Most likely, it was caused by the smell of dinner that came wafting down the corridor. Either way,

## JUNE 13, 1902 BALTIMORE, MARYLAND

he started to salivate. Then, he heard several doors open and the tramping of many feet along the hallway. Oddly, he heard no voices, just the tramping of feet. Jidgie got up and peeked around the corner where the sound and smells emanated. The sight surprised him.

Just then, his father emerged from the office with another man who was wearing a black costume. Jidgie started to laugh at the brother's cassock when a stern glare from his father stopped him.

"George, this is Brother Dominic. From now on you will obey everything he says, or there will be hell to pay!" With nary a goodbye, Big George pivoted and walked out of his son's life.

"Please come into my office, George. Welcome to St. Mary's Industrial School for Orphans, Delinquent, Incorrigible and Wayward Boys," said Brother Dominic, the headmaster. His tone was genial, quite the opposite of his father's. It was the first time he could remember anyone using the word please when addressing him. Sensing a need for calming reassurance, the man placed his hand on the boy's shoulder and drew him close.

"Have a seat," said the man, gesturing for George to take a large chair, while the man sat opposite him on a low-slung wooden stool.

"I know that the name of this place can be imposing, so, why don't we just call it St. Mary's or the Home?"

A wary Jidgie nodded.

"My name is Brother Dominic. I run this place. Actually, to be more accurate, I run this school. But, it's not school like you know it. It's a special school for special boys like you."

Jidgie's shoulders relaxed a little bit as his eyes wandered over the shelves of books.

"Yer office looks like a bookstore. I ain't seen these many

books . . . ever."

Brother Dominic chuckled at the boy's innocent charm. "Listen, George, you are welcome to come to my office at any time to read a book or just come to visit."

"Brother, I'll be honest with you. School and me don't get along. I just can't stand being cooped up, ya know."

"Well, son, things are different here. We teach you how to behave and you will learn a trade. Remember, we will always be there to help you."

"Always?"

"Yes, *always*."

George slumped and cast his eyes down at the brother's emphasis.

"Is this a crowbar hotel?" he asked.

Brother Dominic looked amused at the slang term for jail.

"Well, yes and no," said Brother Dominic with a smile.

"Your father has asked us to take care of you for a time. So, you cannot come and go as you please. You will follow the same schedule as the other boys – mass, class, training, and recreation each day. He said that your mother is not feeling well. Your recent behavior with . . . Oinky, was it? had a bad effect on her and she needs some rest. So, your father has asked us to take care of you. Consider it a vacation of sorts."

"What is a vacay . . . whatever that word was you said?"

"A vay-cay-shun is a holiday, a time away from everyday life. You will be at St. Mary's for a month. After that time, we will meet with your father to discuss your status."

"Just my father?" asked Jidgie.

Brother Dominic nodded solemnly. The boy deflated.

After a pause, Jidgie asked, "Do you think it was wrong to bring Oinky into the house? She was scared to death during that hail

## JUNE 13, 1902 BALTIMORE, MARYLAND

storm and I had no choice. She might a' drownded chained in the shed like that," said Jidgie, his voice rising, his eyes searching. It never occurred to him that the pig might have caused his mother any distress.

"George, you will find St. Mary's is very much different from Pigtown. Here, we try to think about what will happen before we act."

A confused look came over Jidgie's face.

Sensing that the youngster was having trouble grasping his new reality, Brother Dominic said, "I'll bet that you are a little overwhelmed and a lot hungry. Why don't you and I grab some supper? Then, we can get you settled into the dormitory. The dining hall is this way."

Jidgie sighed and thought that maybe things were about to improve.

The dining hall was filled with hundreds of boys seated by age – the youngest in the front. When Brother Dominic entered with Jidgie, the din of conversation subsided. All the boys rose. Brother Dominic led them in grace which they repeated half a beat behind him. The boys crossed themselves and sat. Off to the side was a series of tables filled with bowls and utensils, and mounds of fresh bread and caldrons of soup. Jidgie marveled as the boys filed, table by table, through the food line. The oldest went first.

Jidgie squirmed, fearing that the food would run out. Invariably when the supply dwindled, a team of men would replenish the dishes. Finally, it was the turn of Jidgie's table. He took his tray and filled it with delicious smelling food. After a harrowing day, at last he relaxed while filling his neglected belly.

Later, Brother Dominic escorted him to the dormitory and his bed. There were beds arranged in dozens of rows across a large open bay. Next to each wrought iron frame bed was a chair for each boy to place his day clothes on. The sheer expanse of the sleeping area in comparison to his cramped bedroom in the apartment over the saloon stunned Jidgie.

The room quieted as a tall man in black clapped the boys to attention. After reciting several Hail Marys and one Our Father, he led them in a brief goodnight prayer ending in

". . . if I die before I wake, pray the Lord my soul to take." The room became dark.

Jidgie pondered the final words of the prayer and shivered. He longed for his own bed and the happy face of his little sister breathing softly across the way. Instead, his ears were inundated with the sounds of snores, coughs, and farts. An overwhelming sense of sadness washed over him and he started to cry. Muffling his face into the pillow to avoid attracting derision, he released all the fear, sorrow and loneliness that he had been repressing since his father collared him outside the schoolyard. A burning rage against his father filled his mind. He missed his mother, Mamie and all the Bunnies, even Gunny. He feared that he would never see them again. Little did he realize that he was about to encounter the person who would have the greatest influence on his life.

"There, there, no need to cry. It may seem dark and lonely at this moment, but someone greater than us all has great plans for you," whispered the brother who had hall duty that night until the night watchman came. The immense hand of Brother Matthias softly stroked the youngster's back. Jidgie pulled his face off the pillow to see a gentle giant of a man whispering tender words of encouragement to a scared little boy.

Brother Matthias was an imposing figure, standing 6 feet 5 inches tall. He was the prefect of discipline at the school. The black cassock, highlighted by the ever present cross wrapped around the waist that the Xaverian Order wore, hid the musculature of the young cleric. Born in Cape Breton, Nova Scotia, some thirty years earlier, Brother Matthias devoted his life to converting hardened delinquents into productive citizens. Brother Matthias was a towering figure to the boys. As might be imagined with a population of 800 troubled boys ranging from youngsters like Jidgie to young men almost 21 years old, the potential for fights and violence was high. Stories about how his mere entrance upon the scene acted to defuse volatile, potentially violent situations were legion. The residents of St. Mary's simply called him "Boss."

He was a humble man of faith who believed that idle hands were the devil's workshop. Consequently, he filled St. Mary's with a constant regimen of physical activity; specifically, baseball. He oversaw the forty-four baseball teams at the school. Many a graduate of the Home credited Brother Matthias for inspiring them with his devoted coaching and prodigious displays of power.

Although the "little field" where the Colts of the youngest division played was hard and littered with sticks and broken glass, the boys of St. Mary's played baseball incessantly – often as many as three games per day. Brother Matthias was a talented and tireless coach. He insisted that each boy learn to play every position on the diamond so that he could substitute as needed in a pinch. The most oft-repeated memory was of the exhibitions he would put on after supper on Sunday evenings when he would propel baseballs high and far into the night swinging a fungo bat with just his right hand. The entire student body would scramble after the bombs that came off his bat. Matthias would conclude by rapidly hitting so many balls in the air that, ". . . the balls kept falling down like snowflakes over the entire yard."[ii]

"Listen, George, I know that St. Mary's can be overwhelming at first. However, trust me, you will fit in soon enough." The round-faced boy, eyes red from crying, had a dubious look on his face as he looked at his comforter.

"I don't belong here, Brother, I don't fit in. These guys have their own friends. My gang is back in Pigtown," said Jidgie.

"I know that it might seem that way to you now, but give it some time. Soon, you will have so many friends here that you won't be able to remember all their names," said the brother.

"You know, I'm not good at remembering names now," chuckled the boy.

"Do you like baseball, George?"

After an enthusiastic nod, Brother Matthias continued. "Tomorrow we have tryouts and you can join a team according to how good you are. Would you like that?"

"Yes. You know, Brother, I'm pretty good at baseball."

"I'm sure you are," replied Brother Matthias. "Now get some sleep. We get going really early around here. Mass is at 7:30 A.M. Don't be late. Just follow Jonas, here, he'll take care of you."

The boy in the next bed waved and whispered, "I'm Jonas. See you in the morning."

George acclimated quickly to the baseball fever at the place fittingly called the Home. The beginning of the Babe's phenomenal baseball career was best described by the superstar himself many years later:

'On the second day in school, I made the Colts, the smallest ball team in the institution, as a catcher, and it was only a couple days later that I stepped up to the plate with the bases full, measured a nice groove ball and socked it over the centre-fielder's head for the first home run of my career. My smack won the ballgame, and I stood high with the team . . . .

## JUNE 13, 1902 BALTIMORE, MARYLAND

Since that day I have put over a good many home run wallops, but no drive I have ever made meant half so much to me as my first home run at St. Mary's.' iii

### ● ● ●

The days lengthened, summer solstice came and went. Jidgie settled into the routine at St. Mary's and adjusted exceptionally well; no doubt, in part, due to the summer schedule which was notable for being short on academic classes and being long on baseball. After a few transgressions, mainly having to do with tobacco – smoking and chewing, George began to understand what was expected of him. He did not want to disappoint the Boss. Jidgie's month-long stint at St. Mary's quickly came to an end.

At the same time that young George prepared to return to his home above the saloon on West Camden Avenue, there was a dramatic change in the newly-formed American League that would have a profound impact on Ruth's future career. In July, 1902, American League President Ban Johnson took control of a struggling Baltimore franchise and relocated the team to New York City for the 1903 season. Initially called the Highlanders, the team later became known as the New York Yankees. For the first time, the American League boasted of a franchise in New York City, the baseball capital of the world.

When he came to pick up George at St. Mary's in mid-July, the first words out of Big George's mouth were, "Your mother has gotten much better since you've been away. Make sure that you don't cause her any trouble, or I will make sure that you never get to play with your buddies ever again."

Jidgie clenched his jaw and waved goodbye to Brother Matthias and his friends at St. Mary's. His time there had been one of the best times of his young life. Brother Matthias saw something unique in the outgoing youngster and tried to impart some discipline into the boy's life. The Boss had a way of giving his undivided attention when he explained something. He would spend time with the boy explaining how things were interconnected; something that Big George never did. The only instructions Big George gave were frantic and at a high decibel, often a hodgepodge of English and German.

His mother and sister were waiting for him at the curb. They rushed him and showered him with hugs and kisses while Big George stood there woodenly, grasping the neck of his son's pillowcase. All the boy did was cause trouble and he was welcomed home like the prodigal son. All Big George did was work day and night to keep his family from starving. Where was the fairness in this world?

The welcoming concluded abruptly when Big George announced that his son had a ton of potatoes to peel for the evening's dinner. He marched Jidgie into the kitchen and threw him an apron. Jidgie was crestfallen. Once he settled in to the chore, he decided to stave off boredom by moving the peeled potato bucket to the opposite side of the room and proceeded to throw curves and fades with the peeled potatoes. He never missed.

Back in Pigtown, away from the watchful eyes of the Xaverian Brothers, he soon regressed. Without the structure of early morning mass followed by vocational training and then baseball, Jidgie became restless. To satisfy his restlessness, he reverted to his prior delinquent behavior. This, in turn, caused his mother to suffer anxiety and physical distress.

JUNE 13, 1902 BALTIMORE, MARYLAND

Image of St. Mary's Industrial School early 20th Century

Brother Matthias and Babe Ruth (1920s)

# 4

# 1902
# Baltimore, Maryland

> "If it wasn't for baseball, I'd be in either
> the penitentiary or the cemetery"
> ~ Babe Ruth

"Plop! Plop! Plop!"

Tomatoes rained down on the police wagon that was cruising along East Pratt Street. The Bunnies were armed with a case of over-ripe tomatoes that they had pinched from Giacomo's Produce on the edge of the Little Italy section of Baltimore's Inner Harbor. The Bunnies had taken their ammo and were perched on the roof of one of the tenements common to the area. Jidgie had admonished his boys not to hit the horses; but wait until the wagons were directly below and then aim at the roof of the police vehicle.

Of course, Gunny bridled at Jidgie's instructions and wanted to display his superior tomato-throwing skills. In his haste, one of Gunny's throws went awry and struck one of the steeds on the flank causing the horse to lurch forward. Instead of ducking out of sight, Gunny watched in perverse delight as the driver struggled to regain control of the wagon which careened down the crowded avenue knocking over peddlers' carts.

# 1902 BALTIMORE, MARYLAND

"There he is!" shouted a man on the street, pointing to Gunny. He stood frozen just like he had been the week before by a train's headlamp when the Bunnies were scavenging in the B & O railyards. Then, an alert engineer had seen him and blew the train whistle. Gunny had nearly jumped out of his skin. Now, there were whistles of a different sort.

Stash huddled behind the rampart covering his ears from the loud, shrill sound of police whistles that echoed through the neighborhood.

The coppers rained shouts of, "Halt!" "Stop!" "We're going to arrest you buggers!" on the Bunnies. Jidgie was the first one to react.

"Let's get outa here," he shouted. "They are climbing the stairs. We gotta get to the next roof! Come on!"

The boys followed him, jumping from one roof to the next. The policemen yelled epithets at them, but, were relentless in their pursuit. The officers were red-faced. Their whistles were silenced by their lack of breath. As they closed ground, they grew angrier and brandished their nightsticks. Jidgie feared that the Bunnies were about to get caught and be brought back to their parents. That would not be pleasant. He had to get them out of this mess. His options were dwindling and his heart sank when he saw that the next rooftop was the last. A huge chasm lay beyond the next rooftop. They would be trapped and surely apprehended. He could hear police reinforcements following the progress of the chase along the street.

Wide-eyed, he searched the horizon for a miracle. Suddenly, an answer appeared. A door at the rear of the next roof opened and a hooded figure emerged with wind-milling arms trying to get their attention. Jidgie thought that he was imagining a rescuing angel. He hurtled the last parapet, the rest of the Bunnies close behind. They raced toward the door. It slammed shut behind them, leaving the police to bang and kick at it. They were in a dimly-lit, small space. A rush of foul air enveloped them. For a fraction of a second he thought it was the smell of rotten tomatoes. Then, he realized that it was garbage. Jidgie wondered whether or not they had just gone from the pot into the fire. The outer door would not hold for long. Shouts from below signaled the presence of police entering from the street. They were doomed.

"Quick, come here, into the dumbwaiters," whispered the angel.

Later, back at the Bunny Hole, Jidgie would recount the horrified, facial expression of each Bunny as they squeezed into the two tight conveyances on either side of the cramped space. Once all the boys were tucked inside, the dumbwaiters were lowered slightly and Jidgie and the angel jumped onto the top of each device and pulleyed them downward. The dumbwaiters reached the basement with a thump.

The Bunnies ran out the back exit to escape into an alley. Behind them they heard bewildered shouts of the coppers trying to figure out where the miscreants had vanished. Their precise verbiage was not as bad as the language used by their sergeant when he learned of their ineptitude.

A combination of adrenaline and excitement propelled the Bunnies to their hideout. They tumbled through the entrance and were overcome by relieved hilarity. They could not stop laughing. When they were safe inside, Jidgie counted noses. All were present and accounted for; except for the addition of the rescuer.

Jidgie approached the hooded figure and extended his hand.

"Hey, thanks. Without you we would have been scorched muffins. Really, thanks."

An awkward silence was followed by a shy handshake.

"Yeah, I figured that you needed to ditch before the coppers got to youse guys. I'm Colina, by the way."

Pulling back the hood, she shook her hair out. Except for Gunny, the Bunnies were speechless. Just as Gunny started to berate Colina for violating the Bunny code against girls, Jidgie cut him off.

# 1902 Baltimore, Maryland

"Gunny sit down and shut up. It's your fault that we almost got caught. I'm not going to let you insult our new friend just because she is a girl. My Mom and sister are girls and they are good people. Welcome to the Bunny Hole, Colina."

They spent the rest of the afternoon with introductions and regaling their guest with tales of adventure. When the final cigar stub became unsmoke-able and the lone growler was empty the Bunnies drifted to their homes. Jidgie decided to walk Colina to her home. It turned out that she was from New York City and was spending the summer with relatives who lived on Stiles Street.

● ● ●

Two days later, Jidgie found himself on Stiles Street. He had the strangest feeling, one he had never felt before. He just had to see Colina again. He did not know why; maybe it was the feel of her skin when they shook hands that captured him. He could not rid himself of the image of the delicate eyelashes that fluttered before hazel eyes when she laughed. Maybe it was her daring and ingenuity in fashioning the escape. Jidgie liked the way she drank from the growler without first wiping the rim, or, the way she did not bother that some root beer dribbled down her chin. Unfortunately, there was no one he could talk to about these feelings. The Bunnies would mock him and his family members would dismiss him. Maybe Brother Matthias could help, but he was so far away.

As Jidgie entered the alley that led to her apartment, he hummed to himself. Suddenly, he was struck dumb. He thought that he heard the voice of God. A sound so melodious and powerful flooded his ears. Jidgie stopped in his tracks and smacked his palm against the side of his head. He must have hit the water too hard when the boys were diving off the pier earlier. Jidgie hopped on one leg trying to release the water that must be in his ear. The heavenly sound continued.

"Why are you hopping around on one foot?"

"Eh, what?" Jidgie responded, reddening at Colina's voice at that moment.

Colina giggled at the strange behavior of her new friend. A small air-pop escaped from her lips as she tried to suppress her chuckle. She leaned out of the window and gazed at him with a look of profound amusement. Jidgie looked back at her and pointed to the window.

"What is that amazing sound?"

"That? Oh, that's *Signore* Caruso, the world's greatest opera singer."

"He lives with you?"

"What?"

A look of comprehension illuminated her face. "No, no, that's *Signore* Caruso playing on the Victrola."

It looked like Jidgie's eyes were about to cross. She asked, "You've never heard of a Victrola before, have you?"

As Caruso's voice rose to a crescendo, a mesmerized Jidgie shook his head blankly.

"A Victrola is a machine that plays music. We put a black platter on it, crank it, and the most beautiful sound comes out the front. Come on in and I'll show you," she said pointing to the door.

The first thing he noticed when he entered the ground floor apartment was the Victrola. It was a quarter-sawn oak cabinet with a curved wood top that was hinged back in the open position. Caruso continued to serenade them with his expressive singing. Jidgie felt light-hearted as Caruso professed his love. Although Jidgie did not speak Italian, he felt the anguish and sincerity that Caruso expressed for his forbidden love. Colina beckoned him closer, pointing to the black shellac record spinning on the turntable. A sharp needle held in a circular cartridge tracked across the surface of the disk. Colina grasped two door handles and moved the doors in and out, widening and narrowing the opening in the front of the cabinet. Jidgie broke into a grin with the change in volume as Colina manipulated the doors.

"Do you mind, cuz? I'm trying to study here."

"Oh, Soldano, I'm sorry. I was just showing the Victrola to my new friend Jidgie," said Colina.

"I don't give a rat's petooty. You've been warned to leave the machine alone while I'm studying. Now, start the record over and go away . . . quietly."

Jidgie was unable to see the source of the voice which emanated from the shadows of a dark corner. From the robust, commanding voice, he imagined a large presence. Colina gestured for Jidgie to follow her through a swinging door into the kitchen. The day was filled with sensory surprises. Almost immediately saliva filled Jidgie's mouth. The aroma of garlic, basil, olive oil, and other spices simmering in a rich, tomato gravy overwhelmed his nostrils.

"What is that incredible smell?"

"It's my *Zia Nilly's* tomato gravy. Wait until you taste it," said Colina.

She pulled him over the counter where there was a loaf of bread. Ripping off the heel and another piece, she handed him one.

"Now watch," Colina said, as she dipped her bread into the gravy. It came up steaming and dripping. She blew gently until it was cool enough to eat. She took a huge bite, a clump of gravy dripped down her chin. Before it fell, her tongue rescued it. With a satisfied smile she said, "Now it's your turn."

Jidgie hesitated, then plunged his slab of bread into the pot. His fingers recoiled from the heat of the gravy. Jidgie watched forlornly as his bread floated like the white tip of the mast of a sunken schooner in a sea of red. Colina guffawed by his side.

"Not to worry, *pagliaccio*, clown," she said, fishing the distressed bread from the gravy with a large fork. The only evidence of their surreptitious tasting was a flotsam of bread crust floating on the surface of the bubbly gravy. With her hand under the gravy-soaked bread, Colina blew it cool.

"*Ecco,* here it is." Colina fed it to him. His eyes widened with delight.

"Holy Moly that is the best thing I've ever eaten!"

As Colina giggled, a busty woman dressed in a plain, black dress entered the room. She was short and her face bore a familial resemblance to Colina.

"This is my *Zia* Nilda, her name means 'warrior woman.' The family calls her Nilly."

"What's going on in here?" she demanded. "Who's been scarfing my gravy with my bread?"

Her face was stone-cold expressionless as she moved toward Jidgie. A wooden spoon circled in the air. Suddenly, she rushed past him and plunged the spoon into the gravy and stirred it until the tiny bubbles of steam disappeared from the surface. She turned the gas knob to the left and faced him. Jidgie stood frozen, eyes wide open. Before he could react, her arms encircled him and she kissed him on both cheeks.

"*Benvenuto!* Welcome," said Nilly.

Then, turning to her niece she commanded, "Colina, you and your friend set the table. We're going to eat in ten minutes. Soldano, go wash your hands, *Mangeremo in dieci minuti.*"

● ● ●

Summer ended and school resumed. Jidgie resented the intrusion on his adventures. The truant officer changed tactics. Instead of harassing George over the whereabouts of his son, the officer pestered Katie constantly about Jidgie. This coincided with a profound deterioration to her health. Her coughing spells now were punctuated by bloody spittle which she tried to hide in handkerchiefs that were stuffed into the pockets of her aprons.

Previously, she had tried to cajole her son into behaving. Now, she grew harsh and irascible when he disobeyed. After a particularly bad week, she caught him sneaking into the apartment close to midnight. She snapped.

"That's it! You are going to learn to mind me, boy!" She berated him as hard as she could with her hands flailing through the air like a whirligig that had lost its moorings. Suddenly, her hand struck the door jamb and, there was a loud crack. Katie screamed and fell to floor crying.

It was a good thing that Jidgie stayed away until the next evening because the Ruths spent most of that night in the hospital tending to Katie's wrist. Big George fumed about his wife's misfortune and the extra work it meant for him until she recovered. They made up their minds that Jidgie had to go. Big George scrounged up the tuition and dragged him back to St. Mary's in November.

Life in the Ruth household was tumultuous even without Jidgie's antics. Big George and his wife quarreled about many things; mostly about the liquor inventory which seemed mysteriously prone to shrinkage. Tension between the couple erupted into a public argument at the annual ball held by the Jolly Brothers.

"Listen, Katie, I want you to take it easy tonight. No tippling," said George as they entered the Maennerchor Hall on Lombard Street. The dance committee had transformed the stodgy meeting place into a winter wonderland, reminiscent of the homeland his parents had described to him when he was a youngster. If they couldn't afford to travel to Germany this was the next best thing. Tastefully decorated in holly and greens, the normally staid hall was bright and festive. An Ompah band entertained the guests with traditional German folk songs. Across the hall was a replica of the Drachenfels mountain with a medieval ruin on top, just like the real scene that had been memorialized by Lord Byron in verse. This had been built by George and his fellow choristers and would serve as the backdrop for their performance later in the evening.

"I'm serious. Let's enjoy ourselves. Your sister Lena is babysitting Mamie and we have the night to ourselves."

With a petulant shrug, Katie nodded.

The Hall was noisy and packed with many people from the neighborhood. The annual ball signaled the advent of the Yuletide season. William, George's brother, beckoned them to a table filled with friends and family. Katie settled into conversation with her sister-in-law, while George and Will went to fill their plates with food from the buffet table. Billy Tickner, a Ruth Saloon regular, joined the table and soon was engaged in animated conversation with Katie. George was so engrossed in the festivities that he failed to see Billy pouring from a silver flask secreted in his jacket into Katie's cup. As the evening passed, the decibel level increased, most noticeably in the laughter of Katie and Billy.

"It's time, George. Our quartet is due to sing next," said Fritz, the burly baritone who led the Jolly Brothers Quartet. George and the others went backstage and donned *lederhosen* for their performance. From offstage, they began singing a German drinking song while they marched onto the mountain. The crowd gasped with delight at their costumes and soon were clapping and thumping in time with the music. With a huge smile spread across his broad face, a sense of well-being enveloped George increasing with each rousing chorus. It had been quite a while since he had felt this good.

He wanted to share his exuberance. George's eyes searched the room for his wife to no avail. Despite his smile, worry lines appeared on his forehead. Then, he saw her in the back of the hall. He blinked in disbelief. Katie and Tickner were hugging. George bolted off the mountain and raced to his wife. He grabbed her arm and dragged her out into the cold night.

"That's it. I've had it with you," said George.

"Bufft, George, I . . ." Katie slurred.

"*Halt die Klappe*! Shut up!" said George.

The next morning George whipped open the shades to awaken his still-intoxicated wife.

"Get up! Lena will be here with Mamie any minute now."
Katie squinted through her fingers and moaned.
"I'm going to meet with the lawyer. We are selling this place and moving you away from temptation."

And so it was that the family moved lock stock and barrel to South Hanover Street, east of the Camden Yards terminal. When Jidgie returned to his family in time for Christmas 1902 after a month-long stay at the Home, it was to a new location. He was as confused as his baby sister by the change in circumstances. Again, his family occupied an apartment above the saloon. Jidgie would joke later in life that, "'When I wasn't living over it, I was in it, soaking up the atmosphere.'"[iv]

For now, he would remain in Baltimore and experience several dramatic events before returning to St. Mary's and Brother Matthias in 1904.

Baltimore, Maryland early 20th Century street scene (circa 1906)

# 5

# February 7, 1904
# Baltimore, Maryland

*"A small spark neglected has often kindled a mighty conflagration."*
~ Quintus Curtius

He woke up this Sunday morning feeling pretty good about himself. It was the day after he had celebrated his ninth birthday. His special day had been pleasant. There had not been a single dustup with his father all day. The family had enjoyed a good laugh when Jidgie unwrapped his presents consisting of a new pair of sailor pants and a thick Navy peacoat and his father had remarked that he was growing so fast that he would soon wear man's clothing. It was a truth attested to by his overstretched overalls that rode up his legs stopping at mid-calf.

It was also true that he had hoped for a new leather finger-mitt to use for his obsession – baseball. But, he had to admit that he needed the clothes, so he hid his disappointment. He all but forgot about the baseball glove when all the patrons at Ruth's Saloon sang a somewhat drunken Happy Birthday to him. And when the men

## FEBRUARY 7, 1904 BALTIMORE, MARYLAND

threw pennies to him in celebration, he scavenged every last one in the hope of buying a leather fielding mitt. Within twenty-four hours, this feeling of tranquility would be shattered by a major calamity.

Sunday was considered a special day in Pigtown because the Sunday Blue Laws prohibited most forms of commerce so that Sunday could truly be a day of rest. For Jidgie, it meant that Ruth's Saloon was closed for business. Sunday mornings were relatively peaceful while the family attended church. His father was less volatile, although he still busied himself in the early afternoon inside the saloon cleaning and making repairs until it was time to go to Katie's parents for Sunday dinner.

On this day, Jidgie got his father's goat by suggesting that the family attend mass at St. Peter the Apostle instead of the habitual services at the old Otterbein Church on West Conway Street. Katie could sense that Big George was about to unleash on the boy. She defused the situation by leading the family toward the Otterbein.

"George, don't let him get your nanny," Katie said smiling.

Later, as they walked back from services, Jidgie held his mother's hand while his father carried Mamie. It was a cold and windy day and the smell of smoke and wisps of ash like an evil imitation of snowflakes began to fill the air. Jidgie wiped at his eyes. A slight, white haze suffused the sunlight. Almost simultaneously, the smell of burning wood filled their nostrils. In the distance they heard sirens.

"*Feuer*! Fire! Katie, take the *kinder* home. I'll be right back," said George.

Heading toward the commotion, George turned and admonished his son, "Jidgie, stay with your mother and Mamie."

52

Back at the saloon, Jidgie climbed to the roof of the shed to observe the chaos in the streets. Big George sent word that he had joined a bucket brigade and would not be home until the fire had been tamed. The sun waned and a noticeable chill settled over the burning city. The residents of Pigtown trafficked in rumors throughout the day. Rumor had it that fire departments from as far away as New York City had been summoned. Another was that the loud booms that they heard earlier in the day were dynamite charges that had been exploded in an unsuccessful effort to halt the progress of the fire.

Katie saved the *Baltimore Herald* from the day after the Fire. The paper reported that the damage consumed sixty to eighty blocks destroying some fifteen hundred buildings and more than twenty-five hundred businesses. The *Herald* cautioned that, given the chaotic state of communications, the early estimates might not be reliable.

It was rumored that the fire was caused by the careless discarding of a lit cigarette in the basement of John E. Hurst & Co.'s wholesale dry goods house. The smoldering fire eventually reached a gasoline storage tank that exploded, sending flames and burning embers to adjacent buildings. Adverse wind conditions and bad luck contributed to the sweeping advance of the fire. Shortly after the fire began, Fire Chief George Horton was incapacitated when he touched a sparking electrical wire, thereby depriving the Baltimore Fire Department of effective leadership to combat the fire.

While his father was still working the fire brigade, Jidgie was standing on the roof of the shed, mesmerized by the unfolding tragedy. The fire was moving from west to east giving him a prime view. His face was smudged black by the commingling of ash with tears from his smarting eyes. His coat was speckled with fire residue.

## February 7, 1904  Baltimore, Maryland

Suddenly, the shed rocked. He barely kept his balance. His attention was drawn to a dark figure below him. A hairy back pushed against the frame. A grunt followed. A broad smile creased his face. He jumped down to greet his friend.

"Oinky, how did you find me? Scared by the fire, huh, girl?" said the boy as he knelt to tousle her ears. He was dumbfounded over her ability to locate him in the chaos after all this time. Then he remembered hearing a story told by a sailor in his father's saloon about a pig that had such a great sense of smell that it crossed the Swiss Alps to find its master.

Oinky must be one of those pigs with that uncanny ability he thought to himself. Oinky had grown, but her hide felt taut and was tangled with spiky burrs. His fingers touched the stump of her tail. The pig responded by rubbing her face against his chest and neck.

"I'll bet you are starving. Stay here while I get you some vittles," said Jidgie quietly. He was so happy to see Oinky. He figured that she had lived a feral existence in the many alleys and wooded areas around the city. He had overheard men in the saloon telling tales of beasts such as alligators, snakes, and orangutans that lived in the shadows. Baltimore was an active seaport and rail hub and he had seen many different animals unloaded on the docks and railyards. With all the pigs that were herded through the streets, it made sense to him that some might escape and survive out of sight.

Jidgie tried to act casual when he entered the house. His mother and sister were upstairs glued to the window watching the fire. He raided the icebox and brought Oinky a bowl of water. While she guzzled appreciatively, Jidgie formulated a plan. Certainly, Oinky was too big to hide in the shed. His father would not abide her presence. He had to act quickly.

Fashioning a leash from a piece of rope, he looped it around

Oinky and then led her through the neighborhood to the trolley stop. After a few minutes, he saw a trolley approaching. How could he get her onto the trolley? A thought popped into his head and he covered Oinky with his peacoat. The trolley screeched to a stop and Jidgie nonchalantly climbed aboard. He avoided eye contact and poured all his pennies into the glass fare receptacle. The operator looked at the coins spinning noisily, looked in his mirror at the empty vehicle and looked at the boy and the pig in the coat. He chuckled to himself, what the heck, the boys at the depot will never believe it.

"There's room in the back, son. Take your sister back there out of sight."

Jidgie started at the reference and looked up toward the smiling driver. After a beat, Jidgie got it and smiled back. The boy and the pig sat dutifully, except when the trolley rounded the curves on the way out of town and Oinky lost her balance. She squealed until Jidgie righted her and hugged her tight.

When they reached their destination, the driver gave them a cheerful wave. With the trolley disappearing in the distance, Jidgie stood at the curb wondering whether he had miscalculated. The front door was so far from the street that it felt like he was entering another world as he approached it. The front of the building was dark. He walked to the alcove and stood before the massive wooden door. It was locked. No doubt everyone was in the dining hall for the evening meal. Sunday suppers were always a special occasion.

He heard a noise inside and banged at the door.

"Hello, hello. Can I see Brother Matthias? Hello," shouted Jidgie.

"Who's there?" was the response.

"It's Jidg . . . George Ruth, . . . the catcher for the Colts."

## FEBRUARY 7, 1904 BALTIMORE, MARYLAND

"OK, stay right there."

Oinky looked up at Jidgie who was shivering in the winter air. He was blowing on his hands when he heard the Boss striding toward the door. When he opened the door, his gaze fixed on the coatless boy. Matthias immediately shed his own sweater and bundled it around the boy and ushered him into the warm foyer.

"What do we have here, George?"

Jidgie burst into an incoherent torrent of explanations, excuses and fears. Matthias listened patiently, gleaning the essence of the problem.

"I think I have a solution to this problem. Let's tie Oinky to the railing right outside. In the morning, I will bring her to a farmer friend of mine. In the meantime, why don't you join us for dinner?"

Jidgie hesitated. Although his stomach was rumbling, he knew that he had a long walk home ahead of him. He had thrown all his pennies into the coinbox on the trip out and had no money for the fare back to town.

"It's Sunday. We have weiners, your favorite," enticed Matthias.

Jidgie wiped a dribble of saliva from the corner of his mouth. The thought of weiners, or tube steaks as his father called them, was too much to resist. The boy nodded, "OK, as long as I can bring one out for Oinky."

"Deal," chuckled Brother Matthias.

⚾ ⚾ ⚾

The reports of the damage from the fire got bleaker with each passing day. The property loss toll exceeded $150 million. To avoid a run on the banks, the Commonwealth of Maryland declared the ten business days after the fire to be legal holidays. There was a remarkable absence of reported deaths and soon a mythology developed that no lives had been lost. In actuality, several firemen from other locations died from subsequent pneumonia and other illnesses related to exposure to the fire. Aside from the devastation to property, the cruelest effect of the fire was the consequent loss of over thirty-five thousand jobs.

Mayor Robert McLane who, at thirty five, was the youngest mayor in the city's history, tried to rally the citizenry with brave pronouncements. He told the *Baltimore News*:

"'Baltimore will now enter undaunted into the task of resurrection. A greater and more beautiful city will rise from the ruins and we shall make of this calamity a future blessing. We are staggered by the terrible blow, but we are not discouraged, and every energy of the city as a municipality and its citizens as private individuals will be devoted to a rehabilitation that will not only prove the stuff we are made of but be a monument to the American spirit.'"[v]

He then refused financial assistance from the federal and state governments, stating:

'As head of this municipality, I cannot help but feel gratified by the sympathy and the offers of practical assistance which have been tendered to us. To them I have in general terms replied, 'Baltimore will take care of its own, thank you.'

'To suppose that the spirit of our people will not rise to the occasion is to suppose that our people are not genuine Americans. We shall make the fire of 1904 a landmark not of decline but of progress.'

● ● ●

The focus of all Baltimoreans in the wake of the Great Fire was on survival and reconstruction. Except for Katie's remarking about the disappearance of a large slab of shepherd's pie, Jidgie's sojourn to St. Mary's and back had gone unnoticed.

## February 7, 1904 Baltimore, Maryland

Jidgie's heart ached as he watched the health of his frail mother deteriorate. The smoky air damaged her lungs and stamina. She spent many a day without leaving bed. He was too young to comprehend the extent of her problems. The youngster tried to fill the void around the saloon, but constantly butted heads with his father.

Jidgie devised a solution.

"Mama, I got a job today."

"What? You're talking nonsense. You're only nine years old."

"So? You always tell me to act like a man. I can earn money for us."

"How? Are you going to be a child model, *gutaussehenden jungen*, my handsome boy?"

Jidgie blushed. His speech became agitated at his mother's failure to take him seriously.

"Mama, I want to help. I can sell newspapers to make some money. Don't try to stop me. I already signed on to deliver the *Herald* each morning. My route has twenty-five customers and I can use a dolly that I found by the stockyards to carry the papers."

"*Ach!* Look at this one. So grown up," said Katie, with tears welling up in her eyes.

At the time of the Fire, the city editor of the *Baltimore Herald* was twenty-three-year old H.L. Mencken. He was undeterred by the conflagration and managed to publish the *Herald* in borrowed space of other papers in return for photographs his staff had taken. After publishing the paper disembodied from its offices on the northwest corner of St. Paul and Fayette Streets and not getting home for a week, Mencken quipped that he '. . . went into the fire a boy fueled by the hot gas of youth, and emerged almost a middle aged man, spavined by responsibility and aching in every sinew.' [vi]

Once the immediate crisis passed, he realized that all the newsstands in the downtown area had been decimated and that the paper needed another means of reaching its customers. The distribution system he devised was to hire young boys in Baltimore's neighborhoods. Jidgie was among the first hires of what Mencken referred to as his army of urchins. And so, Jidgie began his career as a door-to-door delivery boy for the *Herald*.

After several weeks of early rising and delivering newspapers in the rain, sleet and snow, Jidgie's route doubled in size. He was punctual and reliable. Since the neighborhood was home to laborers and dock workers, many of the men left for work before dawn and before the newspaper was delivered. Jidgie saw an opportunity to hawk newspapers in the afternoon on the corner across from the Otterbein Church on West Conway Street. Katie was concerned that he was working too long and too hard at such a young age. Despite her fears, Jidgie would not be deterred. She was amazed and impressed that he followed the rigorous schedule. Then, in the blink of an eye, it all came crashing down.

One evening in the dwindling light, Jidgie found an old wooden box and decided he could use it as a table for the papers he was hawking. He astutely recognized the demand for an afternoon paper that the workmen could read at the end of the day. It helped that he knew everyone in the neighborhood and enjoyed chatting and exchanging stories with them. He liked working in front of the brick church which functioned as a crossroads for the working class.

The temperature was barely above freezing, but the raw wind and freezing rain coming from the Northeast penetrated his outwear. The sky was steel gray with a blanket of low altitude clouds that promised more freezing rain. A brisk wind rippled the newspapers that were held in place by a large beige rock atop a sheet of plastic covering the papers on his sturdy wooden box.

He was wearing the navy blue knit cap that his mother knitted and had given him for Christmas. It was pulled down low over his ears. He pulled the flap of his pea coat up to his neck and secured the top button.

As winter changed to spring and spring to summer, the economy rebounded. The cost of the *Herald* was one cent. With the impact of the Great Fire fading and a new optimism emerging, Jidgie noticed that some workmen began dropping nickels in his collection jar, an old Ball jar.

Throughout the spring, the Bunnies gathered after supper to play baseball until they could no longer see the ball in the dark. As their level of play improved, they received challenges from other neighborhoods. Little Italy was east, on the other side of the Inner Harbor. That neighborhood boasted a strong team, but, largely due to Jidgie's prowess, they were unable to defeat the Bunny team. The previous evening, Jidgie had trolley-wired a ball that one-hopped into the harbor to drive in the go-ahead runs and win the game.

That evening, Jidgie was wearing denim overalls and a sleeveless T shirt. He had his mother's expressive eyes that sparkled with mischief and intelligence. He wore a workman's cap that his buddies had given him. His full lips were bright red from the cup of cherry Italian ices Jidgie had just finished. He was chewing the pleated paper cup trying to squeeze the last morsel of flavor out of it and imagining the upcoming night's heroics, when he heard the whiny voice of Carlo.

He was six months older than Jidgie and was a grade ahead of him. Carlo was a husky boy with a large physique, broad shoulders and large hands and feet. He was like a clumsy puppy that had yet to grow into his adult body. His face was pimply and ruddy. He had pig eyes and a dull countenance that made him seem perennially a half a beat behind the others in any discussion. His black hair was helter-skelter on his head as if he had combed it with a mechanical eggbeater. Carlo was wearing a T shirt with a hand-painted logo of the Baltimore Orioles of the Eastern League across his chest and long blue dungarees that were marred with holes and patches. Jidgie eyed him with a degree of amusement because Carlo was the pitcher in last night's game who had delivered the meatball that Jidgie deposited into the harbor on a bounce.

"Hey Jidgie, you little Kraut punk, you got lucky last night. Wait 'til tonight."

Jidgie glared at him with a smug look and said nothing. Seeing that the younger boy was not intimidated, Carlo snatched the money jar from the wooden table.

"I guess I'll just take the money for a new ball from your money jar."

Jidgie grabbed for the jar, but the taller boy held it out of reach over his head, taunting the younger boy, calling him a Mama's boy. Carlo noticed that Jidgie was unfazed, so he upped his attack and called Katie an expletive.

With lightning quickness, Jidgie shoved Carlo as hard as he could. The jar flew out of his hands and smashed into a thousand pieces when it hit the sidewalk. Before additional blows could follow, Rev. Jürgen, who had been watching from the window, sprinted from the rectory and separated both combatants.

Carlo was crying. Jidgie's chest was heaving and his eyes were

## February 7, 1904  Baltimore, Maryland

ablaze with fury. Pastor Jürgen admonished both boys that fighting was a sin and they should shake hands and forgive each other. Jidgie initially refused, saying that he did not need to be forgiven. Eventually, the pastor prevailed and he sent Carlo on his way. Pastor Jürgen helped Jidgie pick up the coins and scattered newspapers.

Jidgie packed up his belongings and headed home, deflated by the ebbing of adrenaline from his bloodstream. His mother was waiting for him with a look of maternal concern. He collapsed before her and hugged her legs, releasing pent up tears into her skirt.

"Oh, Jidgie, I heard. I heard from the neighborhood gossip. But, why did you have to shove him?"

"Mama, he called you a nasty name."

"Do you know what that nasty name means?"

"No, but I know it's bad and that you are not one!"

Tears slid down Katie cheeks as she knelt down and drew her little man close.

"Don't worry. Don't worry. *Ich liebe dich*, I love you."

# 6

# 1904
# Baltimore, Maryland

> "He was the greatest man I've ever known,"
> ~ Babe Ruth

The saloonkeeper was in the basement of his establishment busy setting up the kegs of beer, which had been delivered that morning. His wife called for him to come upstairs. There was a sense of urgency in her voice that told him that it was not an ordinary call to him to help move a crate of potatoes.

There were two men standing by the door when George Ruth emerged through the trapdoor leading to the basement.

"What can I do for you?" he asked.

"Good morning. We are city inspectors. We received a complaint about your establishment. We will probably be here all morning. We expect you to cooperate. We will start in the kitchen. Please gather all your records on sanitary practices."

"What records?" said George incredulously. He looked to his wife who shrugged her shoulders and gave him a quizzical look.

George eyed the officious men, thinking that this was unusual. When they had completed their inspection and handed him a list of violations as long as his arm, he fumed. He pulled the taller man aside and asked what this was really about. The response nearly sent him through the roof.

His blood pressure continued to rise as he waited for Jidgie to return home from his game down by the docks. George pounced on Jidgie the moment he entered the saloon.

"Boy, you really have crossed the line this time, you little *rotz nase*. You will pay this time, you snot-nosed kid."

Jidgie took a step back, glancing over his shoulder for an escape route. "I didn't do it, Pa."

"Is that so? Are you telling me you didn't shove a boy named Carlo?"

Jidgie paused, the stammered, "Well, yeah, I did but he deserved it. He called Mama a nasty name."

"Do you have any idea who Carlo's father is?"

"No."

"His father is a bigwig down at city hall. His name is Don Tomaso."

Jidgie's blank expression, accompanied by shrugged shoulders conveyed his answer.

"Well, guess what, mister smarty pants, he wants to arrest you for assault," said Big George, waving an official-looking piece of paper in the boy's face.

Jidgie did not know what that meant, but knew that getting arrested was not good.

"We have to go to court on Wednesday to explain to the justice of the peace why you should not go to jail."

Three days later, Jidgie and his father appeared in court to answer the charges. When the Ruths entered the dingy courtroom, the justice of the peace was in a foul mood. Twenty years in the juvenile part had ruined his digestive system and stamped a permanent scowl on his pasty face. Judge Wilford Dernigan sat behind a rickety desk on a platform at the end of rectangular room in the lower level of a rundown municipal building not far from the waterfront. He wore a sweater and a coat under his shiny, threadbare robes to ward off the chill. The constant humidity plagued his joints and caused his once-sonorous voice to come out as a wheezy bark.

Lime from seepage caked the snot-green walls which had not been painted since the building was built shortly after the War of Northern Aggression, as Dernigan referred to it. With arthritic fingers, he fiddled with the stack of folders on the desk. Dernigan was waiting for the clerk-bailiff to return from the bathroom down the corridor before adjudicating the cases on the docket. In the meantime, he spit a glob of saliva into the spittoon and glowered at the pitiful souls before him.

Jidgie had never been inside a drearier place. Not only was there a faint smell of urine and sweat, he detected the scent of fear. With false bravado, he walked through the courtroom with his chin up and a slight smirk on his face. Big George followed, with eyes downcast to avoid eye contact with several of his patrons. There were no available seats in the back rows, so, Jidgie and his father moved to the front where there was some space. George pushed his son by the scruff of his neck toward a seat, grumbling for him to wipe the smirk off his face, or, he would be sorry. Jidgie stumbled noisily into a spot on the bench.

His confidence dissolved as he surveyed the room. Unfamiliarity coupled with uncertainty engendered doubt and confusion in his juvenile mind. As they waited, Jidgie looked at the judge's scrawny ankles covered in argyle socks that were visible under the desk. The diamond pattern of the socks turned Jidgie's mind to his favorite game and he passed the time day-dreaming about his next conquest on the baseball field.

The complaining party had made sure that their case was at the end of the calendar. During the hours of tedium, the only break in the tension came when someone in the fourth row let loose a noisy fart. Jidgie giggled until his father stared him into silence. Gradually, the crowd thinned until the room was almost empty. Every time Jidgie fidgeted, his father bumped him back to order. Big George did not see Don Tomaso enter and stand in the rear of the room. Dernigan barely lifted his gaze and nodded slightly before calling the case of "George Ruth, Jr." Following the examples of those who were called before them, the father stood and pushed his son forward to face Dernigan who barely acknowledged his presence. Big George stood silently behind his son.

In what passed for a proceeding, the judge read a litany of charges and sworn witness statements, then, asked the Ruths if they had any defense. When his father shrugged, Jidgie stammered that Carlo was a sore loser who called his mother a nasty name. Dernigan's head snapped up, "You will not use such language in my courtroom."

Then, with a glance toward Don Tomaso, the Judge admonished, "In my experience, there are more than a few women of that description in Pigtown."

After a long pause, Dernigan continued, "Therefore, it is the opinion of this court that George Ruth is incorrigible and vicious and beyond the control of his parents. I order that said individual be committed to the legal guardianship of the Order of the Xaverian Brothers until he reaches the age of majority. The respondent, that is you son, must report to St. Mary's Industrial School no later than . . . ."

He paused to consult a calendar.

". . . no later than, Sunday, May 22nd, nineteen hundred and four."

The clerk-bailiff sprang to his feet and shouted to an empty room, "All rise. There being no further business before this court, we stand adjourned until tomorrow morning."

Jidgie stood uncomprehending, with his eyebrows knotted. Big George was stone-faced as they walked home. He rebuffed any attempt by Jidgie seeking an explanation. The boy followed quietly, wondering what would happen next.

The elder Ruth wondered how Katie would react to the news that her only son would be taken from her to live with the Brothers for good. She had already lost five children to premature infant death; but, this was worse – it would be like a perpetual open wound with her son gone, but living four miles away. Her health was so fragile that her husband feared the effects of this decree. He had expected a brief detention, or, work on some city clean-up crew. He was floored when the sentence was announced. Although the boy gave him fits, he had noticed some improvement since the boy had been at St. Mary's the previous year. George fully anticipated that Jidgie would help pick up the slack around the saloon as he matured. Commitment to St. Mary's definitely came as a shock.

When they arrived home, Katie was bustling around the kitchen preparing for the evening traffic.

"What took you so long? The first wave will be here any minute now. *Snell, snell.* Jidgie wash the pots."

She saw the worried look on her husband's face, but there was too much to do. They would discuss it later. Jidgie seemed subdued and lacked his usual animation. There was no time to dwell on whatever happened, the family must pull together now.

Although Katie Ruth had a generally angular face, the recent travails involving her son seemed to melt whatever fullness there was. Indeed, she was thin to the point of emaciation and was bothered by a persistent cough. Running a tavern in working-class Baltimore was exhausting. Alongside her husband, she worked tirelessly – cooking, cleaning, and holding her fragile family together – often well into the night, only to rise at dawn to do it all over again. The toll of five infant deaths often left her crying herself to sleep. Big George provided little comfort; he was stoical and, in her estimation, had more than enough to worry to him without burdening him with her frailties. Her only source of solace had been her mother. Since the death of her mother several years earlier, Katie had increasingly found relief from her troubles by drinking too much.

The fateful date arrived quickly. Katie straightened Jidgie's collar as she looked soulfully into his eyes.

"Don't worry, Jidgie. You know the brothers this time. They will take care of you. You will be only four miles away. Mamie and I will come to see you every Sunday we can, won't we Mamie?"

"Yes, Mama," said his little sister. She was crying and hugging her favorite possession, her raggedy Teddy bear that her godmother had sewn for her last Christmas.

"Oh, Jidgie, don't go. Who will protect me when the thunder storms come? Mama, Jidgie is the only one who comes to me when I get scared in the night."

"Don't worry, kiddo, ol' Teddy will and besides I'm not far away. I'll be here when you need me," said Jidgie with a tear in his eye. "You know, pretty soon the summer baseball season will start and you and Mom can come and watch me smash the ball. I'll hit a homer for youse. I will."

Katie knelt and hugged her two children, never wanting to let go.

"Let's go," George bellowed. "The trolley don't run all night."

St. Mary's was not nearly as foreboding to Jidgie as it was

when he first attended almost two years ago. When he and his father arrived, Brother Matthias was waiting for them. Jidgie's heart quickened as he settled into the brother's office while his father's footsteps faded into the background. Brother Matthias filled the small, wood-paneled office that was cluttered with file cabinets and papers hung in rows on the walls. Jidgie had never seen so many papers filled with boxes.

"Welcome back, George."

The big man scanned the guardian papers left by the boy's father and then put them into a folder in a file cabinet.

"How are you, son?"

Sensing a different level of formality than in the past, George straightened up in his chair. He felt the need to impress the Boss by embellishing the encounter with Carlo.

"I'm OK, Boss. I just want you to know that Carlo had it coming. He called my Mom a nasty name so I bopped him in the beezer. Wop!" said George, bashing his left fist into his opposite palm.

Shaking his head, the brother gave him a disapproving stare.

"George, we've spoken of this in the past. Jesus does not approve of bopping people in their beezers."

"Even if they insult your Mama?"

"Especially, if they insult your Mama; it's wrong. Jesus taught us that as hard as it might be, we have to turn the other cheek. That means we have to take all insults and slights without lashing out, or bopping beezers. You understand? Promise me that from now on you won't be bopping anyone in the beezer."

"OK, but what if they insult Jesus, then is it alright? Don't worry, Boss, I can handle myself in a knuckle party," said Jidgie

"No, George, it's never alright."

Once Matthias saw George nod in assent, he showed the boy a pamphlet.

# 1904 Baltimore, Maryland

"I want you to look through this pamphlet, George. There are pictures of the different trades that we teach here at the Home. For example, you can train to be a carpenter, printer, shoemaker, electrician, learn the principles of farming and animal husbandry...."

George giggled at the strange word, conjuring up the image of Oinky and one of her friends dressed up in wedding attire, with a pig pastor announcing that they were husband and wife.

The brother continued turning the pages. Suddenly, George jammed his hand into the pamphlet that Matthias was flipping.

"There, that's it. That's what I want to do," he said pointing.

"You want to learn how to be a . . . ?"

"A tailor. Yes, I learned some at me aunt's. She learned me how to sew. It's fun. She said she never saw anyone who could thread a needle faster than me."

"Well, OK, a tailor it is! Now, George, I want you to tell me if you know what these are?" he said sweeping his hand toward the papers covered with boxes.

"I ain't got a clue."

"You do not have a clue," Matthias corrected.

"Yeah, that's what I said."

The man hid a slight smile.

"These, my young gentleman, are the schedules for the summer baseball teams. We have twenty-eight teams playing this summer. Do you think you might be able to play a couple of hundred games before Christmas?"

Young George's beaming smile was all the answer needed.

About a week later, Jidgie was sitting in the dining hall after lunch waiting to be released for recess.

"Hey, Jidgie, you ought to see Brother Herman. He's handing out the mail and there's a letter for you," said Jonas.

"Don't hand me that piffle. I don't know anyone who knows how to write," said Jidgie in a self-deprecating voice. He got the desired snickering from the boys.

"No, I'm serious. Go check with Brother before he leaves."

Jidgie kept a wary eye on Jonas to make sure that he was not playing a joke. However, he could not detect any tittering or suppressed giggles in the group surrounding Jonas. Sure enough, when he approached Brother Herman, the cleric thrust an envelope in his direction with a hearty, "And, for Mr. Ruth, a letter from Master Gunther of the great city of Baltimore."

A perplexed look covered Jidgie's face. Who the heck was Master Gunther? He stared at the letter and it was clearly addressed to him in the smudgy and unsteady handwriting of a juvenile.

Off in the corner he read the letter. It was from the Bunnies, written by Gunny. Jidgie smiled; he never knew Gunny's real name. Everybody had always called him Gunny.

> Dear Jidgie,
>
> The Bunnies miss you. Things are not the same without you. I have tried to come up with exciting adventures, but it is a lot harder than I imagined. You were great at it.
>
> I'm sorry for being such a pain in the butt. I think I get it from my parents who were born in Germany. I feel like I have to do more than anyone else in order to prove myself.
>
> Me and the bunnies want to visit you. The trolley fare for all of us both ways is $1.25. We are saving our pennies and will get out there some day.
>
> Your Bunnies,
>
> Henry (Gunny) and the rest of the gang.

## 1904 Baltimore, Maryland

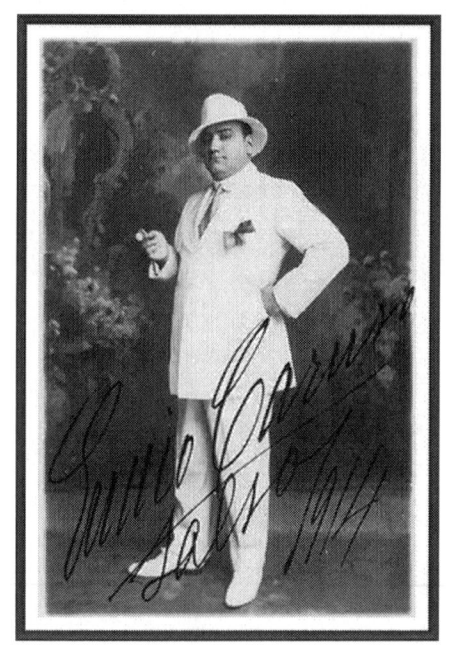

Enrico Caruso

# March 1906
# Baltimore, Maryland

*"Play is the eighth sacrament."*
~ Brother Paul

The next several years were almost tranquil. St. Mary's offered a variety of activities for its charges. Since mass was a daily activity, each of the students received his own hymnal that he retained throughout his time at the school. The daily routine was structured to keep the charges occupied at all times. George attended Mass, then, classes in the morning, learning the skills required to be a tailor. By the time he was eleven, he was a superb shirt-maker, earning twenty cents a shirt. He used his "salary" to buy treats at the school store for his teammates and dorm-mates. For the first time in his life, Jidgie felt valued. St. Mary's served as a haven for the youngster. It would be many years before he learned of the turmoil that roiled all around his family.

Of course, he truly blossomed on the ball field. The inmates, as the boys called themselves, played baseball every afternoon. George developed a special bond with Matthias, who spent countless hours teaching him the game's finer points. Most important, he taught him the value of the hard work of applying oneself to master any skill. The two were virtually inseparable – Matthias carrying a bat and a couple of balls, while George soaked up the nuances of bunting, base-running, and hitting baseballs a long distance. Players on the small field remembered Brother Matthias hitting, pitching and rolling balls at and to Jidgie until neither could see in the darkness. The big man's voice would turn hoarse as he instructed Jidgie with a Canadian lilt, "Keep your feet moving . . . Hands up . . . Butt down . . . Slide step first . . . Never take your eye off the ball, eh." George emulated Matthias' quirky, pigeon-toed running style and his powerful uppercut swing that sent balls heavenward.

Once a month on Sundays in those early years, his mother and sister boarded the trolley and visited him. They often brought him German delicacies that he could not get at the Home. He amazed them by sharing with his friends whatever goodies they brought. The thing that they enjoyed the most was watching him develop into a fearsome and fearless baseball player. Katie would shriek, "*Juhu*! Hooray!" whenever he blasted a home run. Then, she would twist away from Mamie and the field, and dip down toward her purse to imbibe from a flask. On the not infrequent occasions when her son hit multiple homers, she needed Mamie's help to walk to the trolley.

In addition to earning spending money at the tailor shop by virtue of his diligent shirt production, George became a model of stellar behavior – gone were the bad habits, cursing, and fights. When George was eleven, Brother Matthias decided that he was ready for an extended furlough. Unfortunately, there were catastrophic events in the Ruth household that prevented the brother from fulfilling his obligation as legal guardian to try to re-integrate a boy with a family back into family life. So Matthias furloughed George to other situations. These family catastrophes would be kept secret from George for several years.

● ● ●

Back in Baltimore, Big George relaxed in his new establishment reading the paper. Moving his saloon to a more heavily-trafficked location on West Conway Street had been successful. New brass fixtures and the embossed tin plate panels on the ceiling added a modern touch that helped attract new customers. The decree sentencing his son to St. Mary's as an incorrigible had helped also. No longer was he responsible for tuition – it was now paid courtesy of the taxpayers of Baltimore. All-in-all his finances had finally taken a turn for the better. Now if only the rest of his life could be so positive.

His attention turned to the task as hand. The owner of Ruth's Saloon was looking for a bartender. Little did he know as he perused the classifieds how momentous this search would be.

"Listen, Sowers, you come with good references and I'm inclined to put you on. The business is growing and I need the help," said George. He had met the applicant at the annual ball of the Jolly Brothers Club the previous November and had been impressed with his efficient, easy-going style. George tried not to show his desperation; so much depended on making the right choice. Simply put, his wife Katie had a drinking problem. Lord knows, she certainly had reason to drink. Over the last ten years, it seemed like she was either in maternity or in mourning clothes. They had buried five infants, her parents, and George's parents in that time. He was sick of people telling her that parents should never have to bury their children. The doctors had offered no explanations. They kept saying plenty of fresh air and a healthy diet is what children need.

## March 1906 Baltimore, Maryland

They never addressed what to do about the mother. Katie was thin to a fault and had trouble providing enough milk for the newest baby. He was named William, after George's older brother. Although the baby was six months old, he weighed the same as when he was born last August. He was always hungry and crying. Katie was listless and haggard. One of his regulars at the saloon had even commented that the dark circles around her eyes made her look like a raccoon. He got a rousing laugh from the boys for that remark. George made sure that his next drink had a goodly amount of spicy German mustard. The man was too drunk to notice.

Losing that many children in such a short time had strained their marriage to the breaking point. With the help and guidance of her mother, his wife had always been able to cope. However, since the death of Katie's mother almost six years ago, it seemed like the spunk had gone out of his wife. Grandma Johanna's death was so close to the death of baby Mamie's twin sister back in 1900 that Katie never recovered from that double whammy of death.

Just last week he had found her passed out on the sofa with baby William next to her bellowing like a beached sailor. George thought he smelled liquor and he carried her up to their bedroom. Katie's sister Lena came over to help with William, but she was surly and berated George.

"What do you expect? Your wife is in so much pain that only booze makes it tolerable," said Lena. "Why don't you just sell this darn place and go back to selling lightning rods?"

"You know that I can't do that, Lena," he said, recalling his near fatal experience when he slid down the roof of a six story building, only to avoid plunging to his death by hooking onto a gutter. He hung there for an hour until the firemen were able to rescue him. No, climbing on tall structures to install lightning rods was out of the question.

George studied the young man before him. Sowers was not particularly attractive. His over-long hair, lack of facial hair and a puny chin that sloped toward his Adams' apple gave him a decidedly weak look. While the proprietor debated over whether to share his concerns with Sowers, the applicant bit nervously on his lower lip. George concluded that full disclosure would be the better approach.

"There is another subject that we must discuss. My wife is going through a rough patch and has been drowning her sorrows in the sauce too much. I want you to promise me that under no circumstances will you assist her drinking in any way. No matter what she says or offers, she is strictly prohibited from touching any booze. If she even attempts to cajole or beg for a drink you are to deny her and inform me immediately."

"Of course, sir, I understand."

"Then, the job is yours. You start this evening. Report here at 3 p.m. and I'll go over your duties"

"Thank you, sir. I'm looking forward to getting started," replied George Sowers.

With a piercing stare, George followed him as he exited through the swinging door. A sense of foreboding overcame George as he tidied the bar. Was Lena right? Should he return to the lightning rod business that he despised? Should he abandon the only occupation that he was good at? Could he risk Katie's sobriety to this weak specimen of a bartender? As with many of the choices made during his life, George got the answers wrong.

● ● ●

Four miles away, Jidgie was scrunched behind a desk with his chalkboard. Brother Stephen stood at the head of the classroom using a pointer to instruct the students on the finer points of cursive writing. The boys were practicing their lower case letters on specially-lined boards. There was a line halfway between lines to guide the students on the height of loops of the lower case letters. Jidgie's eyebrows were knitted together in concentration. The chalk was clasped firmly in his left hand as he formed a delicate "b."

"Thwack!" The sound of the pointer hitting next to Jidgie's hand resounded through the room.

"Ow, what the . . . ?" cried Jidgie.

"George, you've been told repeatedly that you must use your right hand when writing cursive," admonished Brother Stephen.

"But, I'm left-handed."

"No buts, don't you know that the left is the Devil's hand? Now, erase those letters and re-do the alphabet using your right hand."

This process continued throughout the semester. George became so obsessed with his cursive style that Fats saw him writing inside his hymnal. What he wrote would prove to be prophetic. By the end of the class, George received an award for the best penmanship. So that he would not lose his proficiency over the summer, Brother Stephen provided George with handwriting exercises. He performed them diligently . . . well, kind of. In any event they paid off because throughout his life, he used his right hand to sign countless thousands of autographs with a distinctive, beautiful signature.

"The brothers have informed us that they will be furloughing him for the summer. I just don't know. He's been with the brothers for the last two years. Now, they want us to find him a summer job, but he can't live with us. Does that make any sense?" said an exasperated Katie.

She was seated in the sparse kitchen that had been freshly painted white. She held her head in her hands, resting her elbows on the table top. Her brown eyes welled with tears. Her usually clear complexion was mottled with red splotches from a long bout of weeping. Her brunette hair was pulled back loosely and encircled her oval face. Wet spots dotted her starched white blouse that was open at her throat. Her friend sat across the table trying to look sympathetic. They were about the same age. The two had grown up in adjacent apartments and had been inseparable as youngsters. They were as close as brother and sister.

"OK. Stop crying. I'll take care of him. He's a good kid. School's out for summer. I'll take Jidgie with me to New York. Me and Pasquale have jobs for the summer working with his uncle's restaurant in Little Italy. The kid can stay with us. The three of us can live in the basement of his Uncle Tino's tenement. Jidgie will like it."

"Ok, ok. Let's try it." Katie sighed. "Thanks. Oh, there is one thing that you ought to know about Jidgie," she paused.

"What I wanted to tell you is that he always sleeps with his feet outside the covers. He does not want anyone to touch his feet."

"That's it? I think we can handle that," said Dante, chuckling and shaking his head. "Don't touch the kid's feet. Anything else?"

"Well .... he loves to eat."

"Don't we all?"

"No, seriously, he *really* loves to eat."

"No problem. We'll be working at a restaurant."

● ● ●

On the June day that Dante, Pasquale, and Jidgie arrived in Manhattan, heat waves shimmered off the sunbaked, asphalt pavement. They squinted in the bright sunlight as they searched for

## March 1906 Baltimore, Maryland

Rosina's Restaurant. The trio presented an odd picture. In his early thirties, Dante was a solid six-footer with a naturally muscular physique. He was street savvy and was a worthy guardian for his younger charge. Dante wore a white, sleeveless shirt and faded blue dungarees. His long, black curly hair was greased back and flat-combed in the fashion of the day. His face was clean shaven and masculine with strong, wide features, deep set brown eyes and thick lips.

In contrast, Pasquale Gaetano was short, squat, and flabby. His plaid, short-sleeved shirt was open to his stomach, revealing a thick, thatch of prickly, curly, black hair. Atop his head was an unruly tangle of black hair that had not received the attention of a comb since his last bath about a month previous. His mustachioed face was round, puffy and in a state of permanent amusement reflecting his congenial, self-effacing personality. Pasquale was constantly hungry and was even now prodding Dante, the group's presumed leader, to find the restaurant since they had not eaten in several hours.

Rounding out the band of adventurers was Jidgie, who at eleven years old, was at eye-level with Dante. The boy was lean and lanky with a large boned frame that promised to develop into an impressively proportioned man like his Teutonic ancestors. He had a wide nose and large, expressive brown eyes that, while quick to light up, had a trace of melancholy just below the surface. His baby-faced cheeks were covered with the peach fuzz of approaching adolescence. He wore a pale blue T shirt with a pocket over his heart and the short sleeves folded up to display his biceps. His denim overalls were new and hung down over his scuffed, black boots, indicative of Katie's effort to stay ahead of his growth spurts. His keen vision spotted the sign for Rosina's three blocks away and he nudged Dante and pointed.

After eating a hearty lunch, they went to check out their new digs. Dante surveyed their basement quarters and sighed. It was below grade under a four story walk-up on Second Avenue in Manhattan. To gain access, they had to walk through a narrow brick alleyway, down a flight of concrete steps, through a long, damp, dimly-lit hallway, past the boiler room and the "wine cellar" to a solid metal door. Inside the apartment, the walls were peeling whitewash over the rough stone. The floor was covered with a linoleum tile of indeterminate color due to the thick layer of dust. There were three metal beds with thin mattresses covered by stained linens. A flimsy wooden table and three chipped white enamel chairs were off to the right of the door. Against the wall was a tin-lined oak icebox. Spaced across the concrete ceiling were four incandescent lights in porcelain fixtures with pull strings hanging down. Two small windows seeped gray light from the adjoining alley. A primitive lavatory with a rusted bowl and overhead nozzle for a shower that drained into a grate in the floor was accessible down the alleyway. The good news was that it cost them nothing.

After settling in with their meager belongings, they decided to explore the neighborhood. When they emerged from the building, they heard the buzz of a crowd coming from down the block. Naturally drawn to the noise, they were pleasantly surprised to find a baseball diamond surrounded by cheering spectators. The players were engaged in a spirited battle. The home team was coached by a vigorous young priest in a black cassock with his collar open and wearing a Navy blue cap. The newcomers learned that this was Father Francesco of the Immaculate Conception parish. As they watched the contest, they began to root for the home team in the blue hats. The crowd departed happy, as the locals were victorious, 5-4.

## MARCH 1906 BALTIMORE, MARYLAND

After the game, Dante approached the priest and inquired as to whether his charge could join the team. Father Frank broke into a big grin and said that Jidgie was surely welcome. He walked over to the boy and donned him with his cap and told him that the next practice was the following Sunday after the noon Mass. Jidgie managed a shy smile, thanking the priest. After the Father walked away, Jidgie gave Dante a left-handed love tap in the arm.

"Hey, let's go to the zoo. It's not far," said Dante. Since it was still early, the 'Three Musketeers' as they began to call themselves, headed toward the Central Park Zoo.

"Sounds great!" declared Jidgie.

They walked into the park and meandered past the Arsenal Building, a distinctive structure that in a prior iteration had functioned as a munitions depot. With turrets and other features, the Arsenal was often likened to a medieval fortress. Now, it was covered with ivy and served as the park's administrative center. In the early years of the park, the zoo did not exist. There was only an informal menagerie consisting of animals abandoned by owners who could no longer take care of them. Soon, there were all manner of creatures including snakes, alligators, and goats residing in and around the Arsenal. When the menagerie threatened to overwhelm the Arsenal, the city fathers pushed for the creation of a zoological park. The zoo proved to be an outstanding attraction amid an island of greenery in the middle of the fast-growing metropolis.

It was a delightful afternoon for strolling through the tree-lined paths. Wood log fences helped engender an informal, relaxed nature atmosphere. The zoo was crowded with families walking through the pleasant park and enjoying the animals, both wild and human. After purchasing some Italian ices, the Musketeers went to watch the elephants and marveled at the immense creatures. Jidgie had no patience for the large animals that moved slowly, throwing clouds of dust on their backs to ease the effects of the heat. Jidgie dragged the others to the large circular sea lion pool where they watched the trainers feed whole fish to the barking sea lions. When the feeding was over, their attention was drawn by the frenzied chatter coming from the home of the chimpanzees. Jidgie insisted that they go see what was happening.

Their excitement level rose as they passed fragrant flowers beds that encircled the octagonal chimp cage. The bars rested on a concrete base which was about two feet high. Several large chimps entertained the crowd by swinging on chains hanging from the top of the enclosure. They reminded Dante of the Great Wallendas, the legendary trapeze artists from Germany.

Pasquale purchased some peanuts to feed to the animals. For the most part, the trio threw peanuts to the chimps. Jidgie decided to throw the peanuts *at* the chimps, until an attendant admonished Jidgie not to throw so hard. With that, they began handing the food to hairy outstretched hands reaching through the bars. Jidgie shook hands with one of the chimps and it soon degenerated into a contest of strength. The boy's grip was so firm that the chimp shook loose and scampered behind the tree in the center, all the while chattering a warning to the others in the enclosure.

Across the way on the other side of the cage, Jidgie saw a cluster of people gathered around someone. The center of attention had his back to them, making it impossible to see who was causing such a commotion.

"Who do you think is over there?" asked Pasquale.

"Maybe it's President Roosevelt. I've heard that he likes to bring his kids to this zoo," said Dante.

"Holy Moly," exclaimed Jidgie, "I'd give anything just to say hello to a genuine war hero."

Jidgie dragged the other Musketeers over to the crowd, but his view was blocked. Then, he saw Dante climb onto a bench for a better view.

"Guys, you are not gonna believe it."

"Is it the President?" said Jidgie, jumping up and down to improve his view to no avail.

"No, better!"

"Who is it?" said Jidgie and Pasquale, their voices rising.

"It's your favorite singer, Enrico Caruso."

"The one that Colina's aunt always plays? I love him. He's so powerful," said Jidgie, barely able to contain his enthusiasm.

Jidgie and Pasquale stood on tiptoe in an effort to see the man heralded as the world's greatest singer. He was the premier star of the renowned Metropolitan Opera. Just five years earlier, Caruso had made history by recording the first phonographic record and two years earlier he became the first recording artist to sell over one million copies of a sound recording. He was truly an international star.

The "Great Caruso" was wearing an elegant linen suit with a matching Panama hat tilted rakishly on his large head. He was slightly less than six feet with a compact physique. He had a handsome face, with broad, fleshy cheeks and dark, brown eyes that were at once joyful and mischievous. His large mouth and thin lips were punctuated by a perfect set of ivories that flashed a friendly smile. Caruso was accompanied by a pretty blonde. She was obviously a showgirl as attested to by her painted look and statuesque figure.

Caruso was clowning with one of the chimpanzees who mimicked the singer's every gesture. Enrico started by feeding the chimp peanuts by hand and then escalated to placing the nuts in his pocket and then in his mouth allowing the chimp to take the reward gingerly from wherever it was placed. He dubbed her Bella and the singer and the chimp exchanged contorted looks and made faces at each other. He crooned to her. She responded with a high pitched shriek. The crowd loved it. A pack of reporters surrounded the couple and were busy shouting questions and taking photos of the great singer's antics with his simian fan.

"*Signore* Caruso, we love you," shouted Jidgie. Caruso scanned the crowd for the young voice. His gaze alighting on Jidgie, Enrico responded playfully, *"Venga qui, bambino.* Come here, baby.*"*

With the innocence of youth, Jidgie stepped forward. The crowd parted and he was suddenly face-to-face with the great singer.

"Hey, Enrico, give us a picture with the kid and your girl," shouted one of the photographers.

Caruso smiled obligingly, put the peanuts behind him and turned toward the cameraman with the boy and the showgirl on either side. Just as the flashbulbs popped, Bella pinched the showgirl and she let out a startled scream. The crowd burst into raucous laughter. The show girl's startled expression turned into a look of dismay, then embarrassment, then tears. She struggled to escape the laughter, running down the path leading to the Arsenal.

Bella was perched on a deep branch inside the cage, raining monkey epithets at the girl and throwing peanuts frantically in her direction. All the chimps erupted in a chorus of simian derision. Caruso was doubled over with laughter, with tears of hilarity streaming down his expressive face. Jidgie laughed so hard that he hiccupped hysterically. The crowd laughed and guffawed at the spectacle. They relished the mental picture that would last a life-time and the prospect of a wondrous tale, the recounting of which would be the highlight of many a family gathering.

About five minutes later the girl returned with a police officer and pointed to Caruso, exclaiming loudly, "There. He's the one who pinched me. I want that masher arrested."

The photographers hoisted their cameras for shots of Caruso patiently explaining to the policeman what had happened. He suggested politely that the officer should arrest Bella, not him. Faced with a conundrum, the policeman calculated that arresting the singer would not be well received. He wisely took out his citation book and wrote out an appearance ticket to the singer who graciously sang his acceptance of the ticket and bowed theatrically to the befuddled policeman.

Ever the showman, Caruso made his excuses and, offering his arm to the showgirl, made a grand exit. He was last seen heading toward Central Park South, mumbling something about dinner at the Plaza.

The next morning the face of the startled showgirl filled the front page of every New York tabloid, along with the headline:

## Caruso Denies Pinching Charge, Tells Cop 'Arrest Bella the Chimp!'

# Summer 1912
# Old Bethpage, New York

*"As soon as I got out there I felt a strange relationship with the pitcher's mound. It was as if I'd been born out there. Pitching just felt like the most natural thing in the world. Striking out batters was easy."*
~ Babe Ruth

For the next few years, George bounced around between St. Mary's, St. James Home, and furloughs outside the system of Xaverian facilities. St. James was a Xaverian institution that operated as a halfway house for boys who were ready to transition to post-Xaverian life. It was a halfway house for inmates who got jobs. The superintendent kept their salary in return for room and board. Where a boy was assigned depended on the level of maturity he displayed and the brothers' assessment of his best interests. As one of the more senior inmates, Jidgie was furloughed during the summer in order to gain real-world experience.

As he progressed through his teenage years, he grew physically into a strapping young man. The same could not be said about his emotional development. The vocational training provided at the Home taught him to focus and to complete meticulous tasks. He became a superb shirt-maker and showed promise as a tailor. Despite the discipline of his training, he retained an impish mentality – always looking for a way to have fun. He tended to apply the same level of concentration he had developed in his sewing to his carousing. Once he decided to blow off steam, anything was possible.

His most incredible attribute was the ability to apply an extraordinary level of concentration to playing baseball. One minute he would be joking and guffawing over some practical joke and the next he would be clouting a prodigious drive. His exploits while on summer furlough in 1912 would become legend.

"Well, George, what's it going to be during furlough this summer?" asked Brother Matthias. "The school league will be off until August. I can get you a position at a tailor shop in Fell's Point. They always need tailors to sew sailors' uniforms."

"Brother, my friend Dante has a job for me in the Garment District in New York City. He said that I could work there during June and July. You know that there are too many bad influences and unpleasant memories for me in Baltimore."

Matthias peered over his spectacles at the young man. We certainly are making progress he thought. George would never have even thought of that several years ago.

"Tell Dante to send me a letter from the employer certifying that you have a position for June and July. Once I receive it, I'll make a recommendation to Brother Paul."

Jidgie had another, more compelling reason for preferring New York City that summer. In the back pocket of his overalls, folded in half, was a letter from Colina imploring him to come to the City on his furlough.

⚾ ⚾ ⚾

Jidgie would never forget that Sunday and how fate had put him in Old Bethpage, New York to deliver ice for some fancy party. Dante had asked him to help out at an outdoor picnic for theatre types. Since Colina was working that afternoon in the Restaurant, Jidgie agreed. The extra money would come in handy.

He had made his delivery and had just stuffed the payment he had collected into the pocket of his denim overalls when he suddenly found himself in the grip of strong arms that went under his arms and clasped behind his head. He was in a full nelson and being pressured to his knees. He was momentarily stunned as the realization flashed through his mind that he was being mugged for the money in his pocket. Then, his instincts kicked in and he forcefully lowered his arms while pivoting to his right. As he spun he brought his right elbow into his assailant's ribs as they both tumbled to the ground. Quickly spinning on top of the thug, Jidgie pinned him to the ground when he saw the grinning face of his friend Pasquale.

"Wait, wait, it's me, buddy."

"What the heck are you doing here?" he bellowed in surprise.

"I'm working for Chef Fabrizio, preparing a feast for after the game."

"Jesus, Mary, and Joseph, you nearly scared me half to . . ."

"Listen Jidgie, Chef Fabrizio is the chef for Otto Kahn and this is a big deal party. The reason I jumped you is because we need you."

Pasquale explained that Mr. Otto was an important man at the Metropolitan Opera (he called him a *gran formaggio*, a big cheese). Kahn had challenged Mr. Frazee and the Boston Symphony Orchestra to a baseball game. It seemed that Mr. Otto's team from the Metropolitan Opera won when they first played in Central Park last May. Mr. Frazee then hosted a game in Boston on the Commons. His team won because he brought in ringers from the Boston Red Sox professional team. That hacked off Mr. Otto so much that he bet Mr. Frazee a ton of money that his team would win the rubber match, the deciding game. Mr. Otto figured that he would get the famous Brett "B.O." Oakwood to play for his team.

# SUMMER 1912 OLD BETHPAGE, NEW YORK

"So, Mr. Otto's team should destroy them because B.O. is phenomenal," said Jidgie.

"That's normally true, but check it out," said Pasquale, jerking his head to his right. Jidgie was appalled at the sight of Brett Oakwood under a large oak tree, semi-conscious, covered in vomit and obviously stone-cold drunk.

"The game starts in ten minutes and we have no one to pitch. Do you think you could help us out?" his friend pleaded with desperation in his voice.

"I dunno, Patsy. I gotta return the ice wagon."

"Don't worry about that. Mr. Otto will buy you a new ice wagon if you win. Come." Pasquale took his friend's arm and led him to Otto who was pacing around the drunken ballplayer like an enraged tiger.

"What do you want?" he snarled.

"Mr. Otto, this is my friend, Jidgie, he is a real box artist, a great pitcher. He can pitch for us and beat those snotty bean-eaters."

"Son, we're trying to sober up B.O., but have your friend stick around, in case we need him."

B.O. Oakwood was a tall, rangy man in his mid-twenties. His face was tan and leathery from a lifetime outdoors as a farmer and big league ballplayer. Having grown up in Valatie, New York, he spent many long summer hours tending the apple orchards owned by his family. Tragedy struck his family when he was a young teen. His parents were murdered while visiting relatives in New York City. The culprits were never apprehended. The thirteen year old boy was devastated by the deaths. B.O. was traumatized and angry. He turned to baseball as a release. He played with a ferocity and aggressiveness that, in the words of one local reporter, was "daring to the point of dementia." He thrived as a pitcher who fearlessly defended the inside portion of the plate. His penchant for knocking batters down by throwing 'up and in' earned him the nickname "the

Apple-Bonker" because he aimed for the Adam's apple when he went headhunting on the mound.

Just as legendary as his rage was his drinking. He was a nasty drunk who was known to imbibe moonshine by the quart and fight like a wildcat anyone who tried to interfere. That such a demon would possess incredible talent on the baseball diamond is one of the mysteries of life. There was no question that B.O. Oakwood was one of the greatest ballplayers on the planet – when he wasn't incapacitated by his "elbow problem."

He was slightly bow-legged and walked with an inward slant. His most striking features were the length of his arms and fingers. His wingspan was almost eight feet and served as a launching point for baseballs that approached home plate at speeds up to one hundred miles per hour. His hands were strong and long. He was able to hold six baseballs in one hand. This unique physiognomy gave him a natural advantage in throwing and manipulating a baseball. He was capable of so much rotational spin on his pitches that they swerved and darted like a bull shark. On the mound, he was a left-handed wizard of speed and guile. On this day he was angry and drunk; a potentially lethal combination.

The catcher for the "Ottos", as the Bostonians referred to the New Yorkers derisively, was Frank "Tug" Figaro. He was a stout, muscular fellow who had grown up in Brooklyn Heights working on the docks. Built like a tugboat with a powerful lower body he was able to withstand the rigors of catching. The constant squatting and not a few collisions at the plate had slowed him down over the years, but he was still a formidable presence behind the dish. Laconic by nature, he was a perfect counterpoint for the raucous trash-talk that was the order of the day. In a game dominated by bench jockeys who hurled the most vile insults imaginable at the other team and sometimes their own teammates, he was a model citizen. He could be counted on to keep his composure when others were cursing and brawling. With B.O. drunk as a skunk, it would take all of Tug's considerable skill to keep the game on track and give the Ottos a chance to win.

For the Boston squad, Harry Frazee had loaded it with ringers from the highly talented Red Sox professional baseball team. They were called Frazee's Crazees. Frazee was a theater impresario who had made a fortune producing vaudeville shows. As the United States grew into an industrial nation in the twentieth century and the population began to shift into the cities, Frazee was one of the first to see sporting events as entertainment. He also saw the potential for municipal and regional rivalries personified by local sports teams. What had started out as a casual challenge baseball game between rival musical troupes had turned into a high-stakes contest for bragging rights between two burgeoning cities. The rubber match at Old Bethpage had drawn so much attention in the press that bookmakers had swooped in and were handling hundreds of bets, many with significant monetary stakes.

One of the most aggressive bettors was Karl Muck, the conductor of the Boston Symphony Orchestra. He had been born in Germany and immigrated to Boston in 1906 to become the orchestra's music director. Several of his orchestra members were non-ringers on Frazee's roster. Even though Muck had no understanding of the game of baseball, he was so opinionated and chauvinistic that he believed that everything that he touched was destined to prevail. He bet heavily on Frazee's Crazees.

The field at the Old Bethpage Village was a converted pasture, a rolling field bordered by split-log fences. Temporary wooden stands had been erected along the baselines and in the shade of the massive oaks that lined the streets forming the intersection of dirt wagon paths just outside the village square. A crowd of several hundred spectators had gathered to see many famous and notorious players and musicians strive for the unofficial east coast championship. The crowd was adorned in their Sunday best. Wagons containing refreshments lined the perimeter and the game was taking on the atmosphere of a grand outdoor circus. The remnants of the morning dew made the grass on the field sparkle emerald green in the bright summer sunlight. A pitcher's circle had been cut out of the turf and the pitcher was allowed to release the pitch toward home plate from anywhere in the circle. The umpire stood behind the pitcher's circle and called balls and strikes.

The umpire for that day's game was Chauncey Griggs. He was a gruff Californian who had come East seeking fame and fortune on the stage. Unfortunately for him, he had more talent as an umpire than as a thespian. Nevertheless, he excited the crowds with his exaggerated antics in making calls. Many players resented his gesticulations that often belittled the players. Chauncey cut a dapper figure with his black tails and bright yellow and black checkered waistcoat. The stovepipe hat that topped his large pumpkin-like head, gave him the appearance of an organ-grinder's monkey wearing a diminutive cap. His florid complexion was the result of the heat and more than a few nips from his handy silver flask that was discreetly tucked into his waistcoat.

The crowd was still arriving when the game began. B.O. was in trouble from the outset. He squinted unsteadily at the catcher and unleashed a pitch over his head. That was the sixteenth in a row and forced in a run, and there was still nobody out. Several of the Beantowners had ducked from the high-speed pitches at the last instant to avoid being drilled. The already-tense contest began to take on a new dimension.

A frustrated, inebriated B.O. taunted the bean-eaters and insulted their ancestry in between pitches. And the New Englanders returned the insults in kind. The stridency of B.O.'s invective rose with each unsuccessful pitch. In frantic desperation B.O. turned to the umpire behind him and saw his salvation. He spied the glint of a small, silver flask. B.O. slurred, "Hey, Buddy, ya gotta gimme some hooch."

With an exaggerated motion of fastidiousness, the ump wagged his index finger from side-to-side, gave B.O. a self-satisfied grin, patted the flask in the inner pocket of his waistcoat and said, "You'll never see a drop, you old sot."

B.O. smiled a wicked smile and like a cobra sprang at the umpire, landing right on him. B.O. tore at the waist coat, bellowing, "Give me that flask, you son of a pig!"

B.O. ripped off the ump's jacket and grabbed the flask. With that, all Bedlam broke loose. As B.O. tried to uncork the flask, bodies came flying from all over as the tension of the day erupted. Both managers waded into the pile, and pulled players off. When they reached the bottom of the pile they yanked B.O. to his feet. His left arm hung limply at his side and he screamed in pain. His day and career as a pitcher was done.

The skipper looked at Otto disconsolately. The one thing that Otto detested most was lack of self-control and his disdain for B.O. was captured in his withering stare. As the manager half-carried the injured player to the bench, Otto glanced at Jidgie and nodded. The big youngster adjusted his overalls and stretched both his arms over his head breathing in and out slowly. He leaned from side to side, then grabbed his left elbow with his right hand and pulled it toward his broad chest. Next, he pointed his elbow to the sky and pushed it back behind his head. He held both elbows parallel to the ground and gently rotated his forearms back and forth. The manager dumped B.O. onto the grass behind the bench and handed Jidgie the hand-stitched baseball.

"It's all yours, kid. Don't screw up. Get us out of this pinch."

The scene at the mound was only slightly less chaotic. The umpire was on his feet but he wobbled as Jidgie approached the dirt circle. Griggs' right eye was a swollen mess and blood had clotted below his left nostril. His frilled dickey was splotched blood red and the lining of his torn waistcoat hung down like a jagged flag over his privates. Nevertheless, to the youngster, Griggs appeared to be a tower of authority. As Jidgie threw a few warm-up tosses with the hand-stitched "lemonball", he heard Griggs muttering about the crazy person. Suddenly, he bellowed, "Play!"

Tug got up from his crouch and began walking toward his pitcher. Griggs pointed at him, screaming, "You, you stay behind the plate."

Tug thought better about protesting. He crouched down and held up his gloved left hand and motioned to Jidgie bring it. The next batter was Mick Flanagan, a surly veteran who was a prison guard in the big house known as Sing Sing in Ossining, New York. He had a brief stint as a professional ballplayer that was interrupted by the birth of twins to his sickly wife. A brawny, six-footer, Flanagan had a jagged red scar on his left cheek compliments of a homemade shiv, fashioned by one of the inmates of the high-security prison. That prisoner never caused another problem after Flanagan settled the score. No proof was ever presented against Flanagan, but the prisoners gave him wide berth after the incident.

When Mick stepped to the plate, he spat a stream of juice onto Tug's shoes and slammed his bat on the wooden plate.

"This is going to be fun. Come on, meat, let's see what ya' got, punk" said Flanagan.

Jidgie leaned back and unleashed a rocket directly at the chaw in Flanagan's left cheek. The burly striker froze momentarily and then jack-knifed away, ending up on his arse, with his bat flying toward the third base coacher.

"Ball one," shouted Griggs, suppressing a slight grin as Flanagan dusted off his butt. Tug thought, "Hmmm, this kid has guts." Tug held his glove on the outside corner of the plate and Jidgie delivered the pitch with such precision that Tug's glove never moved.

"Strike one," called Griggs.

The next pitch was right under Flanagan's hands and as he tried to swing or get out of the way, the ball clipped the knob of his bat and rolled weakly toward Jidgie. He pounced on it like a panther, flipped the ball to Tug who stepped on the plate, then tagged a startled Flanagan who was standing there dumbfounded. Tug then zinged the ball to Randazzo at third who tagged a sliding Allie Bushwick for the third out. The Ottos bounded off the field, laughing audibly as the stunned Crazees stood with mouths agape at the turn of events.

As Jidgie strode to the bench he was careful not to exhibit any emotion, keeping a stoic expression. However, Pasquale noticed that when Jidgie got to the foul line he skipped a little higher and his body preened for an instant. By the time he landed, his stoic demeanor returned.

"Kill the ump!" screamed Karl Muck. Frazee who was sitting next to the conductor gave the ump an apologetic shrug. Griggs glared at the pair.

On the mound for Boston was Leo Bilski, a tall, lumbering man of Polish descent who until the previous year was the top pitcher on the U.S. military barnstorming team that travelled from base to base playing teams from the local bases. Leo was thin with a long elliptical face, flat cheekbones, and close-set eyes. The dominant feature of his face was a nose that protruded like a mainmast from the deck of a schooner. The effect of his proboscis was softened only by the bushy red handlebar moustache that rested on his upper lip like a big, furry caterpillar.

Leo made quick work of Johansen and Delany, garnering two quick strikeouts. Tug batted next for the Ottos. Flanagan was behind the dish and signaled for a bean ball. Leo was in the circle and he nodded assent. He and Flanagan had played together frequently over the years and knew each other instinctively. Leo could feel the heat of Flanagan's anger at being embarrassed at the plate and knew that this game had just been elevated to war. He bounced the lemonball lightly with his long, thin fingers and then burst into motion, slinging a fastball behind Tug's noggin. As the missile raced toward him, Tug lurched forward. The ball grazed the back of his head and struck his maroon cap which hung precariously in the air above his recently-vacated head. The velocity of the lemonball knocked his maroon cap all the way to the makeshift wooden curb that had been erected to stop errant balls from bashing into the knees of the spectators. Tug shook his head to gather his wits, inhaled a breath of disaster averted, got up and trotted to first base.

Jidgie, batting in B.O.'s spot, dodged a couple of bean balls aimed at his right ear. With each pitch that smashed into the backstop, Tug advanced a base. Flanagan crouched behind the plate again and signaled for the bean ball. Leo turned to Griggs and asked for a timeout. Griggs nodded and Flanagan sprinted out to the pitcher's circle.

"What the hell are you doing calling timeout?" Mick demanded, "I want to nail that creep!"

Leo said in a low voice, "We can't afford it now. Tug's at third base and if this kid jumps out of the way again, Tug will tie the score. We'll plunk the kid later."

Flanagan looked toward Harry Frazee who shook his head from side to side.

"OK," said Flanagan through clenched teeth, "but we are going to drill him later, ya' got me?" The hurler nodded.

The next pitch was headed right toward Jidgie's ear, he fell down and watched helplessly as the ball corkscrewed back over the plate for a strike.

"Whassamatter kid, ya' nervous?" Flanagan taunted.

Jidgie half-turned toward Flanagan to respond, when he heard

## SUMMER 1912 OLD BETHPAGE, NEW YORK

the ball thump into Flanagan's mitt.

"Strike two!" bellowed Griggs with a wicked grin spreading across his corpulent face.

The next pitch tantalized Jidgie as it bore down on him directly over the middle of the plate. As he swung he whiffed at nothing – the ball darted earthward and was caught by Mick with a barely audible squish as the tobacco juice-covered ball struck the glove. Jidgie was out and Tug jogged in from third, clapping his hands saying, "Don't worry kid, it's only the first inning. Our time will come. We'll get him."

Tug was to be the only base runner the Ottos would have until much later in the game. The gangly righthander for the Beantowners was on that day. He threw an assortment of shoots, fades, spitters, and drops that bedeviled and bedazzled the Ottos. Inning after inning Leo set them down in order. Only two of the Ottos reached base; and they were due to errors. Leo was cruising along with a no hitter.

Jidgie was equally brilliant, throwing slants and zippers with unerring accuracy. In the fifth inning, manager Angus Jackson asked Tug how the kid was doing. Tug smiled and held out his left hand which was swollen and deep purple in color from the incessant pounding delivered by Jidgie's blazers.

Manager Jackson beckoned to Otto and whispered something to him. A few minutes later, Pasquale sprinted toward the bench holding something in folded in waxy, white paper. Jackson handed it to Tug, as he started toward the field. He looked at the package, then at Jackson quizzically. The unfolded paper revealed a slab of exquisite steak. Jackson pantomimed for Tug to put it inside his mitt. Tug shrugged and squeezed the raw meat between his palm and the thin leather glove. He pounded his right fist into his left hand to mold his cushion and trotted to the catcher's box. With each of Jidgie's warm up pitches, Tug's grin grew wider and he gave

Jackson a jubilant thumbs up.

The score stood ominously, at 1-0 in the bottom of the ninth. Johannsen led off and tapped weakly to Leo for the first out. Delany struck out looking. He glared balefully at Griggs as he returned to the dugout. The Ottos were down to their last out.

Up came Tug with two out and the hopes of the Ottos fading fast. Tug could hardly grip the bat as his left hand was so swollen from Jidgie's heaters. Flanagan signaled for an unintentional walk. Leo's eyes flickered a protest, but he just nodded when he saw the streak of hate flashing in Flanagan's eyes. He would not let the day end without revenge for the humiliation of the first inning.

Flanagan called to Griggs for time and sidled out to Leo.

"Listen, Buddy, we're going to walk Tug so that we can get another shot at the gorilla."

"Are you crazy?" exclaimed Leo. "We're a hair away from winning. Let's just end it now."

"Not on your life. You promised me that we would get him and by everything I hold dear, we're going to get him!"

Tug was surprised, yet not surprised, as he watched the fourth pitch sail by wide of the plate. He knew Flanagan's reputation as a vindictive moron. Tug's hand throbbed as he hustled down to first base to watch the drama unfold. Tug calculated that he could still throw a few haymakers with his right hand in the brawl that would surely ensue. Tug rubbed his eyes in disbelief at what he saw next.

Jidgie looked toward Otto and then toward Leo. The youngster suppressed a grin as he pointed with his broad right hand to the pasture out beyond the split log fence in right field. He stood there motionless in the lefthand batter's box, pointing until Flanagan screamed at him, "It's over for you, you dirty dog. Your mother will regret the day she gave birth to you!"

Leo toed the pitcher's line. He did not need a sign from Flanagan. As the lanky pitcher sighted in on the red-faced catcher who had every vein in his neck bulging venomous purple, Leo himself seethed with anger at the busher's brash antics. The angular righthander whipped into his windup and unleashed a screamer right at Jidgie's cranium.

As soon as the ball was hurled, Jidgie nimbly stepped back and swung his bat in tomahawk fashion at the menacing projectile. The collision of the bat with the ball produced a ringing crack and there was a faint smell of burnt wood from the friction of the bat striking the ball. All eyes followed the graceful arc of the meteor that sprung from Jidgie's bat. It rose in an eastward trajectory, high and far over the fence before it thudded one hundred and fifty yards away, hitting Reginald the bull just above his snout, right between the eyes. The massive black creature shook his proud head, lowered it and proceeded to swallow the ball with one slurp of his fat tongue.

The silence after the crack of the bat was broken by Tug who whooped and hollered like a schoolboy as he ran backwards around the bases so he could watch Jidgie gingerly touch each one. The big kid minced his steps as he approached each bag. As he approached second base, the Crazee patrolling that area gave him a discreet pat on the rump. When he reached home plate, Tug was there with a huge hug.

As Jidgie skipped into Tug's arms, a murderous Flanagan threw a roundhouse punch that caught Jidgie on the side of the head with a loud bone-crunching crack.

"We need a doctor here, right away. Help! We need a doctor here, help!"

Jidgie was floating along in a rowboat with the sweet face of mother Katie floating above his, whispering to him. He felt a peaceful calmness as she dipped her hand in the water and sprinkled some cool droplets on his face. "Mama, Mama," he sighed.

Then, he heard a loud, guttural voice, "Hey Kid, hey Kid," and he felt a splash of cold water douse his face. He coughed and sputtered and took a deep breath. He sensed that he was horizontal, lying on the ground surrounded by murmuring people.

As he tried to sit up, he felt a sharp pain radiate through his noggin. In the distance he heard a voice, "Hey, Kid. Are you there kid? Say something?"

Slowly, Jidgie squinted his eyes open. The light stabbed like a white-hot knife searing into his brain. OK, take it easy, you'll be alright. His brain slowly whirred into gear. He began to comprehend that he had been hammered from behind by something or someone. Oh, yeah, it must have been that moron Flanagan. Jidgie now realized that he had been cold-cocked. Someone thrust a cup of cold lemonade toward his mouth. He sputtered noisily and opened his eyes.

A few feet away, Flanagan was on the ground screaming in pain and gaping at the knuckles of his hand. The shattered white bone showed through the dirt-covered skin, as the blood dripped down his wrist. His face contorted in agony as he dropped to his knees, gripping his limp hand with his left. Leo rushed over and screamed, "We need a doctor here, right away. Help! We need a doctor here, help!"

A man in a suit, wearing a derby and carrying a black bag, stepped toward Flanagan and told him to sit against the backstop.

"Get a litter over here right away," the doctor bellowed.

Two young men sprinted to the barn. The man in the derby withdrew a large stethoscope and pressed a funnel shaped implement to Mick's chest. As he did so, the man held Flanagan's right hand upward and splashed it with some liquid from a bottle he had removed from his bag. The big catcher howled as the man in the derby cleaned the wound. Taking some gauze out of the bag, the man carefully wrapped the hand and used the gauze to fashion a sling.

"You have to get to the hospital right away," said the man in the derby, while he looked into Flanagan's eyes for signs of shock. Two boys came rushing up with a litter, loaded Flanagan onto it and dragged him to the hospital wagon that had just arrived at the edge of the field.

"Thanks, Doc," croaked Mick. The man in the derby nodded.

Leo joined his friend in the hospital wagon and noticed as they pulled away past right field that the man in the derby was bending over Reginald trying to remove the lemonball from his gullet. Leo stared at the black bag on the ground and could barely make out the words, "Dr. Simpson, Veterinarian."

Jidgie was on his feet surrounded by Tug and the rest of the team and Pasquale, all grinning at him. The crowd parted and Jidgie was face-to-face with Otto. His eyebrows were knitted with concern and his lips were pursed into an oddly quizzical expression.

"Are you OK? That ruffian was totally out of line. We won fair and square thanks to you."

"I'm fine," said Jidgie, but he wobbled slightly. Otto quickly inserted himself under Jidgie's left armpit.

"Here, let me help you. You are my honored guest and must join us in our victory feast."

And so, the odd pair, the oversized youth and the diminutive financier, hobbled toward the flaps of the awaiting banquet tent. When they entered, a loud cheer erupted. Jidgie's name was chanted in rhythm to the drums of the gaily-clad musicians. It seemed like everyone danced to the tune of Jidgie's name. And so, a celebrity was born. Jidgie straightened, and his face beamed at the adulation of the assemblage.

Otto steered the young pitcher toward the head table and shouted, "A root beer for my good lad and a Chablis for me!"

The team broke into raucous laughter.

The euphoria of defeating a supremely-talented team of major leaguers would come to an abrupt end shortly.

# 9

# August 11, 1912
# New York City, New York
# & Baltimore, Maryland

*"Drink was the cause of it all."*
~ George H. Ruth, Sr.

Back in the City, a triumphant Jidgie went straight to Rosina's Restaurant to report all of the details of his miraculous adventure in Old Bethpage. During the ride downtown, his head began to ache. A combination of the blow from . . . what was his name . . . yeah, Flanagan, and a few too many root beers took a toll on his cranium. He fought the urge to vomit.

When he finally arrived at Rosina's, the restaurant was humming at full capacity and Dante was too busy to talk. Jidgie found his way to a chair near the kitchen entrance where he could watch the staff, especially his favorite waitress hustle in and out. It wasn't long before Colina saw him and brought him a steaming bowl of pasta *fagiole*, macaroni and beans. The meal was restorative. He smiled and motioned toward the clock with a questioning look on his face.

"One more hour," she mouthed while shrugging her shoulders.

"I'll be back later," he pantomimed.

## AUGUST 11, 1912 NEW YORK CITY & BALTIMORE

Dressed in clean clothes, Jidgie returned to Rosina's at closing time. From a hook in the back of the kitchen, Colina switched her apron with her wool jacket. Underneath it, she wore her waitress' uniform, a starched white blouse and black slacks that complemented her girlish figure. Colina tried to disguise her enthusiasm, but she failed. She was so glad to see him that she rushed to him and grabbed his hand. Colina twirled around him and pulled him through the front door. Together they walked down the avenue barely touching the ground.

During their walk, Jidgie provided an animated narrative of the game and his bold winning blast. At Bayard and Mulberry Streets they entered Columbus Park. The green oasis amid tenements opened in 1897 as Mulberry Bend Park and, at the behest of the burgeoning Italian-American population in Little Italy, had been recently renamed to honor Christopher Columbus. The two found a bench in a private area surrounded by shrubbery. Colina enjoyed Jidgie's tale. She laughed triumphantly when he explained how he suckered Leo into throwing the pitch that he launched to the bull yard and cringed when he recounted the blow to his head by the evil catcher. To her, it was great theater, her hazel eyes sparkled in the light from the streetlamp.

When he concluded with a description of Otto's toast, she kissed him. His first reaction was surprise. But, her warmth and the softness of her lips caused him to kiss her back. Then, he pulled away, with the image of a disapproving Brother Matthias haunting his brain.

"What's the matter, Jidgie?"

"I don't know. Should we be doing this?"

"Everybody does it, Jidgie. It's called snuggle-pupping," she said with a giggle.

"I don't know, Colina. I mean, Brother Matthias told us that kissing girls and stuff would spoil our baseball skills," he said without conviction.

"Oh, don't be a flat tire, Jidgie," she said, snuggling up to him. He kissed her upturned face.

Jidgie remembered the token of gratitude given to him by Mr. Otto. When they hugged, the circular object pressed into his chest. His heart was beating fast when Jidgie reached into the front pocket of his overalls and pulled out a gold pinky ring. The symbolic rays of the sun encircled a red garnet in the center of the head. Leaning back on the bench, they were mostly in the dark.

"Colina, I can't tell you how happy I am today. I want to remember this feeling forever. I want you to have this to remember it also," said Jidgie, handing her the ring. She thought his awkward formality was adorable and accepted the present. When she felt the smoothness of the shape, her first thought was that Jidgie had fashioned something from a button in the tailor shop. But its heft told her that it could not be made of shell or bone.

"Put it on."

She placed the ring on her finger and held her hand out toward the light of the nearest street lamp. She gasped. The dim light entered the facets of the garnet and flashed crimson sparks.

"Oh, babe, this is too beautiful . . . where did you get it?"

"During the celebration, Mr. Otto came over to me and pressed it into my front pocket. He said that I deserved something very special."

"I can't accept it," Colina replied.

Jidgie could see a film of moisture reflecting from her eyes.

"Of course, you can. You have to. I can't keep it at the Home. I want you to have it."

His response was smothered in a passionate kiss. Neither realized that garnets are often given to a loved one to heal the broken bonds of separated lovers. This ring would come in handy in the not-so-distant future.

## August 11, 1912 New York City & Baltimore

● ● ●

"Wake up, Romeo. It's time to go to work," said his roommate as he threw a pillow toward Jidgie's head. Thinking it couldn't be seven o'clock already, the youngster squinted and wished he could turn the clock back to his snuggle-pupping with Colina.

When Jidgie arrived at his job in the Garment District, the boss told him to bring up wooden mannequins from the basement. He pulled the iron hook on the door that was flush to the sidewalk. The sound of the door smashing into the brick store front echoed through the building.

"Hey, be careful. We don't want a broken window. Come on, pay attention," yelled Antonio.

"OK, sorry. The wind caught it. It's latched now. Won't happen again."

"It better not!"

The morning's tedium was broken only by the brief flashes of sunlight when he surfaced to carry a form to the curb. His shirt stuck to his back and his wide nostrils were desensitized from the musty smell of the accumulated crud in the basement. The wretched conditions did not dampen his sense of well-being. Infatuation does that, and Jidgie had a serious case of Colina-itis, a term coined by his teasing friend.

The mannequins reminded him of Colina and he wondered what she might be doing. He stood on the sidewalk, daydreaming when he heard the tinkling of a bell. Jidgie sidestepped a young boy riding a bicycle. His thumb flicked the lever on the silver bell with a rapidity that astounded Jidgie. With an air of confidence that belied his age, the boy swung his leg over the seat and trotted to a halt. The boy was wearing a serge uniform and a military-style hat with a band proclaiming Western Union. Jidgie was amused by the officious youngster and stopped to watch him. The boy dropped the kickstand and peered into his leather satchel which also proclaimed the identity of his employer.

Although telegrams had been around for more than a decade, they were not so common that a sense of excitement at this modern novelty persisted. The average person rarely received a telegram, so it was considered an important event. Jidgie wondered who the lucky recipient might be. The messenger straightened his tunic and looked to the number on the door and back to a yellow piece of paper in his hand. Satisfied, he approached Jidgie.

"I'm looking for a Mr. George Ruth, Jr. Do you know where I might find him?"

"You're looking at him."

"Here you go, Mr. Ruth," said the delivery boy, handing the missive over. The boy pivoted and was away on his bike before Jidgie had even opened the envelope. The contents would obliterate all his feelings of infatuation and replace them with an empty sadness.

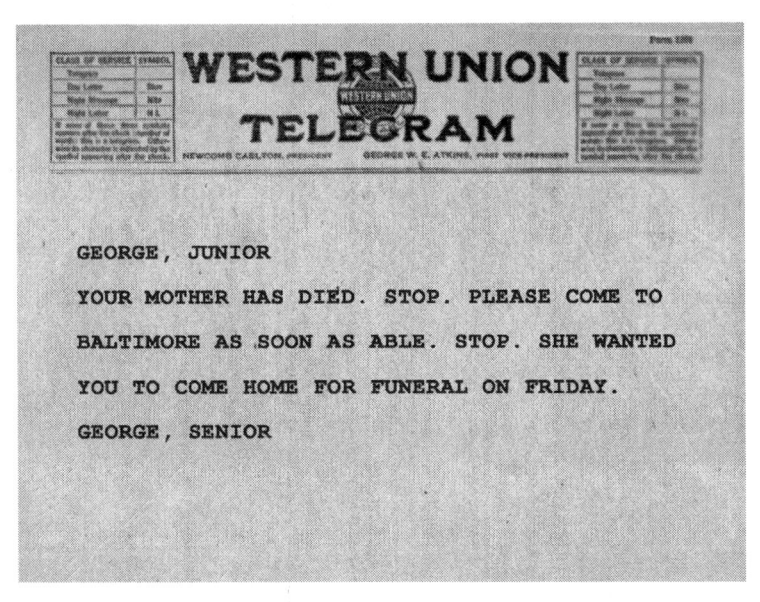

**WESTERN UNION TELEGRAM**

GEORGE, JUNIOR

YOUR MOTHER HAS DIED. STOP. PLEASE COME TO BALTIMORE AS SOON AS ABLE. STOP. SHE WANTED YOU TO COME HOME FOR FUNERAL ON FRIDAY.

GEORGE, SENIOR

Off to the side, he noticed a small whirlwind of grit, paper, and dead leaves emerge from the alley. Swirling unsteadily, it approached him, building as it came. The closer it came, the more intense it was. When it reached him it was almost opaque and spinning more rapidly than one of Walter Johnson's slants. A numbness overcame him as the whirlwind engulfed him. A fetid smell assaulted his nostrils. The roiling debris nicked and scratched his skin. He stared down at his arms. There was no blood; microscopic wounds were outlined with the whiteness of a fish's belly. His skin was puckered as if it had been over-immersed in seawater. The whirlwind surrounded him, concealing the sunlight. Despite his efforts to gain traction with his legs, the whirlwind lifted him and carried him away.

The wind deafened him, reminding him of the time he was caught in the train tunnel with a speeding locomotive as the malicious engineer blared the horn. He rotated with the wind and closed his eyes.

"Jidgie, you must get out of the water. Your skin is pruning."

"It's OK, Ma, I'm ambidextrous," he replied.

"George, the proper term is amphibious," said Brother Matthias.

"Boy, get the hell out of the harbor before I come in after you and make you sorry for disobeying me," screamed his father.

"I can't take it, George. I'm spent. My babies, my poor little babies, six times, how much can a person bear? I'm so tired, so, so tired."

Floating and floating, the wind carried him farther and farther. He was conscious of the noise of a crowd. It grew louder. He heard chanting but it was indecipherable. Then, he was burdened by a weight. His arms ached, he was carrying a body. There was blood everywhere. Tears streamed down his face. He tripped over a stage-light and somersaulted into a pit. It was dark and reeked of staleness. Through blurry vision, Jidgie focused on a yellow piece of paper that he clutched in his hand.

"Are you OK?" shouted Antonio. Rapid footsteps grew louder. Hands grasped him and pulled him to his feet. He wobbled.

"Here, sit on this trunk, *bambino*," said the man. "What happened, *Giorgio*? I saw the messenger hand you a telegram. Then, you were surrounded by a cloud of dust and disappeared. I hear a thud and I find you on the basement floor. Are you OK?"

Jidgie nodded weakly. He handed the telegram to his boss who shifted it to a shaft of sunlight intruding on the darkness.

"Oh, *mio Dio*, oh, my God. I'm so sorry. *Poverino*, poor little one," said Antonio. "Come, we must get you on the afternoon train home. Come, come, get a move on!"

Aboard the B & O Railroad's Royal Blue Line heading to Baltimore, he stared out the train window and watched the countryside whiz past. Occasionally, he stared blankly at the yellow paper in his hand, reading it without comprehending. Before he knew it, he was standing at the station holding the valise lent to him by Antonio. In a daze, he walked through the steam cloud that enveloped the locomotive. The sun was still shining when he emerged from Mount Royal Station. The familiar noise and smells of the street snapped him back. The station was quite a distance from Pigtown, but he walked, partly to clear his mind and partly to delay what was at the other end. Jidgie righted himself and strode toward Ruth's Saloon.

The man behind the bar was washing glasses with his head down when Jidgie entered. His father seemed diminished, smaller and frailer since he saw him last. Jidgie, now, nearly a man, looked at his father with an empty feeling. He felt nothing, just a chill void.

"What'll it be, Bud," said George senior without raising his head.

"Nothing . . . Pop."

The older man jerked his head up and stared at his son.

"How can it be? You look like a man. Where did my boy go?"

He rushed around the bar and grabbed Jidgie by both arms.

"*Mein Gott*, my God, it is you. Jidgie, you made it. Oh, *mein Gott*!"

After a wooden, halting hug, Jidgie was overcome with fatigue. He sat down on a barstool.

"I'm sorry, Pop. It stinks."

"Yeah, ill luck follows the fearful."

"Does Brother Matthias know?"

"Yes. The funeral is tomorrow. Mamie will be glad to see you," said George.

"Where is she?"

"She's with your Aunt Lena on Portland. That's where they've been for a while."

Jidgie gave him a double-take, but, did not to pursue the comment.

"I'm fagged. I need to grab some shuteye. See you later."

Big George shrugged as if to say, it's up to you. Jidgie took two steps and stopped. He felt listless, but realized that he would not be able to sleep. He walked over to a hook behind the bar and grabbed an apron. Rolling up his sleeves, he took a position next to his father and doused a couple of glasses into the hot, soapy water. A slight smile etched on George's face. He felt genuine affection toward his son for the first time in as long as he could remember.

The Ruth men worked side-by-side in silence. Jidgie's mind wandered to his buddy Louis "Fats" Leisman, his bunk mate from St. Mary's. Over the last few years, a friendship between the boys had blossomed. It started with the loss of their fathers. Leisman's had died and Jidgie's had abandoned him. In their loneliness, Fats and Jidgie had often discussed the unfairness that both had experienced. On occasion when Fats explained that his low mood was due to the absence of his father, Jidgie consoled him by saying, "Don't worry, I ain't seen my father in ten years."

In recent years, neither boy had had visitors. Their respective mothers had stopped taking the trolley out to St. Mary's. There was always some belated excuse or reason. The visits dwindled gradually until they ceased without the pretense of an excuse. Jidgie remarked to Fats that the reason Jidgie had no visitors was because he was 'too big and ugly for anyone to come see me.' [vii] He found refuge in baseball and the attention of Brother Matthias. For his part, Fats was predictably comforted by food.

The morning of the funeral came all too fast.

Jidgie dressed in an ill-fitting suit that his father had left hanging from the door of his room. The pant legs were too short and he was too thin for the suit jacket. The collar of his shirt was so stiff that he wished he had the time to sew in his own collar. As he gazed into the mirror, he thought of the disheveled scarecrow in the Broadway show *Wizard of Oz* that he had gone to see with Colina. The memory of her laughter and how she had buried her head into his shoulder when the flying monkeys attacked helped to sustain him.

He wondered how his extended family would react. The last time he saw any of his family he was a boy. Now, at seventeen, he could be described as more of a man than a child. Katie's family was Catholic and had insisted that her funeral be held in a Catholic church. George, Sr. was so overwrought by her death that he lacked the will to resist. He walked with his father the short distance to St. Peter the Apostle R.C. Church. Understandably, his father was distracted and was silent during the journey. Father Quigly met them at the entrance and expressed his condolences. Jidgie looked past the cleric and saw several small clusters of people sitting in the darkness at the far end of the church. There were relatives, neighborhood friends and a few Bunnies in the quiet church. Just as Jidgie exchanged nods with Gunny, a young woman broke from one of the groups and ran toward him. It was Mamie. She was so grown up that, but for the trademark Ruth moonface, he would not have recognized her.

"Jidgie, you made it! Oh, thank God. It's so good to see you!"

She hugged his neck fiercely and cried on his shoulder. At the emotion of his sister, he teared up as well. Mamie hooked his elbow and led him to the front row. He nodded to the relatives and friends sitting around them. His father sat next to them.

The service was short and dreary. Father Quigly recounted his last encounter with the deceased at Municipal Tuberculosis Hospital. He remarked how the death certificate listed exhaustion as the cause of death. The pastor droned on about how her thirty-nine years of suffering was over and she would spend eternity with Jesus in heaven. With the hymn *Amazing Grace* ringing in their ears, they followed the funeral procession to Holy Redeemer Cemetery. A small party returned to the Saloon where a simple lunch awaited.

With Big George dispensing drinks from behind the bar, Jidgie chatted with his relatives. When his Uncle William turned to accept a sandwich from Mamie, Jidgie slipped away to greet a new visitor.

"Boss, I'm so glad to see you. Thanks for coming."

"George, you have my deepest condolences on your grievous loss."

Jidgie spent the rest of the afternoon catching up with Brother Matthias. With a rueful mien, George Ruth watched from behind the bar.

Colina Petronilla (circa 1917)

## August 11, 1912 New York City & Baltimore

Mary Margaret "Mamie" Ruth (circa 1920s)

Babe Ruth as a teenager at St. Mary's
(courtesy of Babe Ruth Birthplace Museum)

# 10

# 1912
# Baltimore, Maryland

*"The cure for anything is saltwater – sweat, tears, or the sea."*
~ Isak Dinesen

The frantic trip to Baltimore from New York had been precipitated by the receipt of the first telegram he would ever receive. The experience was so traumatic that for the rest of his life he refused to accept telegrams. He insisted that family members or friends accept and open them. As his career soared and his fame grew, congratulatory telegrams became common. Even though the telegrams were obviously congratulatory, he shunned them. Rather than open telegrams immediately as most people did, he hoarded them until he was safely sitting at a restaurant with some friends. Only after a few belts of deep breaths was he prepared to hear the contents of telegrams.

His friends turned his telegram-phobia into a game, and they often impersonated the sender in outrageous parodies. Waite Hoyt, one of his roommates in later years, performed a hilarious impersonation of the Red Baron, the fabled German ace pilot who congratulated Ruth on his pitching in a no-hitter. Hoyt whipped a

## 1912 Baltimore, Maryland

red tablecloth from one of the lounge tables and donned a silver wine cooler for a helmet. Hoyt goose-stepped around the bar, pointing at Ruth and screeching words like *weiner schnitzel, wunderbar, and schlort*. Ruth laughed until he cried. These times were in a distant future that the seventeen year old Ruth could scarcely imagine.

Now, he was back in Baltimore in his old room above the bar trying to sort out the rush of events. One minute he was daydreaming about snuggle-pupping with Colina and the next he received a telegram that turned his life upside down. The death of his mother brought to the surface so many memories and questions. Most of the memories of his mother were negative. He could barely recall anything before he was five, but after that his memories were dark and painful. Mostly, his mother was irritable or incapacitated.

Although he had attended funerals before, he knew that the funeral of a parent was different. He was exhausted from the harried railroad trip and the thought of his mother's funeral the day before was almost too much to contemplate.

As he tossed and turned in the narrow bed, his mind wandered to Colina. She had opened so many new vistas to him. He recalled the night that they took their first cruise. She had playfully suggested that they take an ocean vacation. On the appointed evening, she met him at the entrance to the subway. Colina carried a wicker picnic basket that emitted tantalizing aromas. She had to slap his hand away as the train rumbled along the tracks.

"Goody, we are going to make it," she gushed as they approached the Whitehall Ferry Terminal.

Jidgie nodded and followed her as she navigated through the

throng. As quick and agile as he was, he struggled to keep up. At last, she stopped before a turnstile. She put two nickels into the slot and ushered him through to the dock. He was standing at the entrance to the Municipal Ferry of New York, otherwise known as the Staten Island Ferry. The ocean breeze lifted his hair back. He breathed the salt air deeply and smiled. The slightly fishy, stagnant smell of the water sloshing against the pilings of the pier reminded him of Baltimore's Inner Harbor.

Before him lay New York harbor, dotted with sail boats, schooners and even a few steamships plying their way up the Hudson and East Rivers. To his left, loomed the majestic outline of the Brooklyn Bridge. The evening sun gave the granite a brownish hue as it reflected off the metal cables.

They watched a big, lumbering vessel pull into the slip. The gilded word "Brooklyn" spanned the bridge. The twin smokestacks belched smoke as the steam engines reversed and the pilot eased the ferry into the dock. Colina braced herself against him as the ferry thumped into the pilings. He held her close and nuzzled her hair. Amid indistinct shouts, the crew tied ropes as thick as Jidgie's arms to secure the vessel to the pier. The borough flag of its namesake slapped briskly from a flagpole atop the bridge. The metal pulleys on the halyard clanked against the flagpole. Colina pointed at the writing on the flag.

"That's the official motto of Brooklyn, but what does it say?"

"It says, '*Een Draght Mackt Maght*' which means '*In Unity, There is Strength,*'" said Jidgie.

The man next to Jidgie swiveled his head when he heard German spoken.

"*Sprechen Sie Deutsch.* Do you speak German? "

"*Ja*," said Jidgie.

## 1912 Baltimore, Maryland

"*Es lebe der Kaiser!* Long live the Kaiser!"

Jidgie lowered his eyes and grabbed Colina's hand. He briskly shouldered his way through the crowd away from the speaker. They maneuvered to the gangway and boarded the ferry. Colina almost ran to keep up. When they climbed to the second level Jidgie found cushioned seats toward the bow facing their destination.

"Whew," said Colina in a huff, "What was that all about?"

"Nothing."

"Come on, Jidgie, *that* wasn't nothing. We ran like the coppers were chasing us."

"Ok, I wanted to get away from that guy because he praised the Kaiser."

Colina gave him a perplexed look.

"These are dangerous times. There is a major war brewing in Europe, and Germany is right in the middle of pushing for hostilities. It does not look like Germany will be on the same side as America if a war starts."

"What does that have to do with you?"

Jidgie looked both ways, then, sighed.

"Something bad is coming. I just got a letter from my friend Gunny. You remember Henry Gunther from the Bunnies." Colina nodded.

"He told me that thugs on the Baltimore docks have been beating up people who publicly support Germany. Since I speak German, I might be mistakenly targeted as a Kaiser sympathizer. I can handle myself, but I don't want to get into a knuckle party when I'm with you."

"That's sweet, but you do remember that I'm a Bunny and I can handle myself?" she smiled. He gave her a slight nudge of appreciation.

"Oh, look!" Colina exclaimed, pointing to the colorful sunset.

"Holy Moly," said Jidgie.

The two watched the pastels tint the sky. Their heads touched and all was at peace.

When they got to Staten Island, they ambled through St. George's Terminal to the Flats nearby. Jidgie's stomach growled. Colina chuckled as she opened the picnic basket and spread out a blanket.

"Dig in. I got pastrami on rye, knishes, and sour pickles."

"Mmmm, good," said Jidgie, chomping on the thick, over-stuffed sandwich. After he polished off one half, he asked, "What's to drink?"

"Good old Doc Brown's cream soda."

"The best. I wish they sold this in Baltimore."

"Hey, I almost forgot I got good news in a letter today."

"What is it?"

"Remember my cousin Soldano?"

"That whiny little lemon? I remember how he conked it on us to your Aunt Nilly. He told her how we were kissing on the back porch while she was at her rosary society meeting. If you had not made me promise not to throttle him, I would have taught him what happens to snitches."

"Oh, Jidgie, you are a dear." She kissed him on the cheek.

"Back to my news," she said, "My cousin got accepted to the Institute of Musical Art."

"So?"

"All you can say is 'So?'" Colina said, with a distinct edge to her voice.

Jidgie cringed, not understanding his *faux pas*.

"The Institute of Musical Art is just the best performing arts conservatory in the country. It was founded by Frank Damrosch, the godson of Franz Lizst. This is a huge accomplishment. You'll see, someday he will be singing with the Metropolitan Opera alongside *Signore* Caruso."

"I wish him nothing but the best . . . the little snitch!"

They both laughed until their sides hurt.

Sitting on that blanket with darkness encroaching and watching Manhattan light up was one of Jidgie's fondest memories. The future would bring him many highs and lows, it would take him around the world on adventures he could not imagine; but, this one evening would always stand out for him as perfect in its simplicity, purity, and innocence.

During the ferry ride back to Manhattan, they were treated to a spectacular view of the Statue of Liberty under a full moon rising. The ferry slipped through the dark waters while the young lovers stood at the handrail with Jidgie standing behind her, hugging her.

His dream-memory was disrupted by the rattling of the water pipes when his father turned on the shower. It was a new day, a day in which Jidgie would lose another part of his innocence.

## 11

# 1912 Baltimore, Maryland

*When I was a child, I used to speak like a child,
think like a child, reason like a child;
when I became a man, I did away with childish things.*
1 Corinthians 13:11

The morning after the funeral, Katie Ruth's sister Lena was in the apartment kitchen with Mamie before the men had emerged from their bed chambers. After fixing breakfast, she shuffled Mamie and Jidgie off to the living room, so that she would have some private time with her brother-in-law.

"I came by early today to thank you, George. I know this has been difficult for you; it has been difficult for us all. My sister suffered and battled demons. Some of the family members, the ones who don't know the details, are angry with you. But, I've been through most of Katie's suffering with you and throughout you've been most decent."

"That means a lot to me, Lena. When you and Katie were children, you both lost two brothers, then, along came Jidgie, then, Katie lost all those babies. Each death ripped out another piece of her soul. You know how much she grieved – you were there. The only good thing that can be said is that at least her suffering is over.

The rest of us have to make the best of what we have," said Big George, tilting his head toward his son who was chatting with his sister.

Lena Schamberger Fell placed her hand on George's and said, "Will you look at him. He's grown into a handsome, strapping young man. I had a nice chat with him yesterday; he is quite a character. He reminds me of you back in the day. He's so boisterous, alive, and comical. He had us laughing to tears with his imitation of Father Quigly."

"Yeah, well . . . that's just what the world needs – another loud mouth who won't amount to nothing."

"Oh, George, don't be so hard on yourself. What happened to you and Katie was not your fault. Lord knows there's plenty of blame to go around. Maybe it's time to end the cycle of secrecy and lies. Maybe that big kid over there is ready to know history. He might even learn something about life."

With her hand still touching his, she leaned over and kissed him on the cheek.

Deep sadness filled his eyes as he recognized the resemblance Lena bore to his Katie.

"I'll think on it," he said to her as she released his hand and walked over to her niece who was engrossed in conversation with her brother.

"Come on, Mamie, it's time to go. You know how your uncle John gets when we make him wait too long. Bye, Jidgie, don't be a stranger while you're in town. Come by the house, I'll make you a nice home-cooked meal."

"Yes, ma'am, I would like that." He nodded toward the departing figures of Mamie and Aunt Lena.

Later that evening, George climbed the stairs and collapsed on the sofa. His tie had disappeared long ago, as had his shoes. In his shirtsleeves and trousers, he slouched into the cushions with a drink. This was the first time all that day that he was off his feet and it was his first drink. He tipped his glass toward heaven and drained it. He would nurse the next few, but he needed to gulp down the first one.

Now that he was alone and could reflect on Katie's death, he felt a profound sadness. Her life had been a succession of tragedies that drove her to perpetual misery. George winced.

Although six years had passed since that dreadful March day, the wounds were still fresh. Was Lena right? How could he tell the boy about his mother? He poured himself another healthy shot. How could he not tell him about his mother?

The only light in the room came from the fireplace and a string of purple memorial lights that hugged the counter that separated the living room from the kitchen. The fire flickered yellow and orange as it consumed the logs much like the way life consumes us all thought George. His weary sigh sounded almost like the moan of the wind that swept across the harbor after a nor'easter. Jidgie ascended the stairs quietly. He shivered at the mournful sound of his father's breathing.

## 1912 BALTIMORE, MARYLAND

The invitation to sit surprised the young man whose head pounded from the stress of the last few days. Except for the occasional crack or hiss of the fire, silence enveloped them. He thought that his father might have drifted away when he broke the silence in the low, raspy voice of a person who had been crying.

"I loved your mother from the first day I saw her. I loved her through all the good and a lot of the bad. And she loved me and us, even though sometimes it was hard to know. She loved us," said Big George, who slumped into the sofa, a shell of his robust self.

"I guess somewhere deep inside me I know that, but during my life I hardly felt it. Most of the time, I felt that Mama hated me," said Jidgie.

"Son, most of us can only see life through our own eyes - how events impact us uniquely. Sometimes, however, something so bad happens that we get a small idea of what the other person is going through. That's when we begin to understand. I can't imagine all the demons that plagued your mother, but I know that she loved you."

The silence returned. Jidgie thought that this rare conversation might be over. Weariness began to overtake him. Again, Jidgie thought that his father might have drifted off, then, he spoke.

"I think that it's time that you hear the story of your mother's life from perhaps the only person left who can tell it."

A weakened log cracked and shifted, sending a spray of sparks up the chimney. The expanded pile of embers glowed orange. The moon-shaped faces of both men were so similar, yet separated by a generation. Jidgie looked toward his father who stared vacantly at the fire.

"We met in Union Square Park at an Easter egg hunt. I can still picture her over by the Pavilion. She was wearing a lavender dress covered with purple and yellow flowers. Her laugh captured my heart. It was light and infectious. Your mother could light up a room. Over the years as the tragedies mounted, her laughter faded until it ceased to exist."

"You got a girlfriend, kid?" asked the older man.

Jidgie looked at him blankly. From years of practice in hiding his innermost secrets, he instinctively masked his thoughts. There was no way he was going to tell his father about Colina.

"I guess you wouldn't tell me anyway," said George. "Just do me a favor, don't rush into marriage like I did. Where was I? Oh, yeah, then, you came along.

"You were our first child and we cherished you, although I think that your mother may have resented the circumstances of our wedding. Anyway, your mother was always slim and I think the toll of childbirth on her body was too much. In those days, I worked with your granddad and Uncle Will installing lightning rods. Grandpa John was a brilliant inventor and we devoted ourselves to his creations. The family all lived next to each other. The same with your mother's side. I don't know if you remember all the family gatherings with your cousins.

"Then, your Mom gave birth to twin boys. They were small guys and did not last the winter. By the time you was five years old we had lost two more children. I can't explain how devastating it was for all of us. To go through all the stress, excitement of birth and the pain of losing four children in such a short time nearly destroyed your mother. She was always tense and sad.

"She fought with her mother and sister Lena. Your Mom felt that they blamed her for losing the children. I remember one argument where Katie, your Mama, accused her mother because she had lost two of Katie's brothers when they were young lads. They died of paralysis or polio or some such thing. I don't know. I did not know her when her brothers died. Anyway, Grandma Johanna didn't talk to Katie for months.

"I think that's around the time the real trouble started. She would go over to your grandparents' house on Emory Street and your grandma refused to see her. So, she started drinking with your grandpa Pius. He was a queer duck and before you know it the two of them is regular drinking buddies. That's when I decided it was time to move. I thought if she was away from her father she would drink less. After all, she ignored you and you was a handful. Then, came the new century and I thought we could all have a fresh start. By this time, both of my parents had passed and there just did not seem like there was any reason to stay in the old neighborhood; there was too many sad memories.

"Your mother was pregnant again, with twins again. I think

1900 was the worst year ever. Your mother delivered twin girls – Mary Margaret and Augusta, the poor thing didn't last until the summer. Of course, your sister Mamie thrived, but every time your mother looked at Mamie, your mother thought of Augusta and became inconsolable. And then her mother died. Katie took Grandma Johanna's death hard. And by hard, I mean she started drinking harder than ever. Mostly, she drank with Grandpa Pius who grieved the loss of his wife, but your Mama also took to drinking alone. Do you remember as a youngster, all the times we told you that your Mom was in bed sick with a stomach ailment? Well, she was either in a drunken stupor or hungover.

"That's why we had to send you to the Home. You was running wild, I had to work and we was afraid that, hangin' out on the streets, you would get hurt seriously, or worse. I know it was hard on you. It was hard on us, too. We had to pay tuition back then and getting the money was difficult. We sacrificed so you could have a chance."

Jidgie sat dumbfounded. He felt like smacking himself on the forehead. He never realized that his parents sacrificed to send him to St. Mary's. He always thought that it was because they hated him. Confusion, remorse, and emptiness filled him. He wanted to go put his arm around his father. The thought vanished as quickly as it came. Neither the man, nor, the boy could breech that wall separating them.

Big George sipped his drink. He was trying to decide whether to reveal the next chapter. Would his son resent him? Would he believe him? What would telling the whole sordid tale accomplish other than get the burden off his shoulders? In the end, the relative darkness of the room gave him the courage, or was it recklessness, to proceed with the drama.

"You remember how we moved when you were at St. Mary's the first time?"

Jidgie nodded, "Yes, Mamie and I were confused. It was right before Christmas. We always made a game of trying to find the presents, but, in the new apartment we had no chance. We couldn't figure where any hiding places were – the place was pure chaos."

"I guess that is a good summary for our lives at that time. You were gone off to the Home; your mother was obsessed with protecting Mamie from any harm. She did not want to lose her precious daughter to whatever had stolen her other babies. I think losing Mamie's twin sister really unbalanced her. That's when she began to seek the company of other men. Who knows, maybe in her drunken reasoning, it was all my fault – or, maybe she just needed comfort that I could not provide. In any event, when I caught her kissing different men from the saloon I knew it was time to move. That was when we went to the South Hanover place. We stayed there until near the end of 1905 when we moved to West Conway Street.

"After a few months when business was steady, we were able to hire a bartender. I figured that if I hired a bartender, she would not have to be near the booze and would not be able to drink. So, I hired this guy. His name was George Sowers. He was a real noodle, an ugly dummy. I figured that she would be so repulsed by him that she would behave. I was wrong. I underestimated the power drink had over her. I did not think that she would sink that low.

"When I hired him, I made him promise to withhold any booze from her. 'I gave him strict orders not to allow my wife to have any whisky, and also I wouldn't let her go to the store, in order to keep her in the house, so that she would not get any whiskey. To get whiskey, I think she became too friendly with the bartender.'[viii]

"But, your mother was controlled by demons. One day, I entered the bar and they was talking. There was something fishy going on. Katie was constantly after Sowers. I had accused her from time to time of liking him more than me. I was insanely jealous. I should have fired him. Then, the rest would not have happened.

"Can you believe the nerve on that guy? I gave him a job, a good job, too. I let him live in our apartment; he used your room down the hall. Can you believe what a stupid jerk I was? What did I expect?"

Suddenly, the room got quiet except for the sound of sobbing. Jidgie felt a slight chill in the air. He noticed that the fire was almost completely out. Yet, he couldn't bring himself to move. His father poured another drink and composed himself.

"I remember that it was a Monday. I came over to the kitchen and found your mother under the influence of the demon booze.

She denied that Sowers had given it to her, but, I knew that she was lying. I went after him in the bar. He denied it at first, then, admitted that he had left a bottle out for her when he went into the backyard. She took a cupful of whisky. In my heart, I knew that it was much worse.

'... One week later, I filed for divorce against Katie and placed a newspaper ad stating I was not responsible for any debts contracted by my wife. Two months later, Judge Wickes . . . granted an absolute divorce and gave custody of the children to me.[13] It was a few months later that baby William died. He was only a year old. He was your youngest brother, Yer mother blamed me and we didn't speak to each other in the years that followed.

"You probably don't even remember William. He was a cute little bugger. I guess he could not handle being around so much pain. "You was away most of the time and Mamie was still a small child, so we didn't tell you. I don't know if it was right or not. Anyhows, now you know."

## 12

## February 1914
## St. Mary's Lake, Baltimore, Maryland

"People ask me what I do in the winter when there is no baseball.
I'll tell you what I do.
I stare out the window and wait for spring."
~ Rogers Hornsby

When Jidgie returned to St. Mary's the fall after his mother's death, he was befuddled by recent events. Although he had lost other relatives through his young life, this was different. His memories of his mother were checkered. Jidgie remembered her pride and support for his athletic endeavors. These fond memories were tempered by remembrances of shrill and violent tirades aimed at him for some innocuous transgression. Mainly, when he thought of his mother he thought of pain. She seemed so burdened by pain that she could barely function. The revelations by his father of her falling in love with the bartender and the divorce were difficult for him to absorb. He wondered how he would react to a betrayal by Colina. Jidgie wished someone would put these issues into perspective. Certainly, with the finality of his mother's passing there was one less person to help him. He recalled Brother Matthias saying something about time healing all wounds. Maybe he was right.

## February 1914 St. Mary's Lake, Baltimore, Maryland

He was glad that he had reconnected with Gunny. His former antagonist with the Bunnies had grown into a thoughtful, supportive friend. After the funeral, Gunny had visited him at St. Mary's several times. The juvenile competition between the boys evolved into a mutual respect and friendship. Jidgie liked their conversations; they forced him to think beyond the next adventure. Gunny was introspective, where Jidgie was instinctive. Jidgie thought it was comical that Gunny wanted to be a banker; yet, it compelled Jidgie to think about his own future.

Meanwhile, external events beyond his control were shaping his future. In 1912, the world of professional baseball was in the throes of potentially dramatic change. Not since the emergence of the American League had Major League Baseball been threatened by an upstart league. In 1903, the American League challenged the long-established National League for recognition as top level competition. A decade before, the National League had reluctantly accepted the American League as an equal, albeit junior, partner at the table. One of the results had been the end of the season tournament that became known as the World Series to determine the best team in the major leagues for the year. This competition had generated immense interest in professional baseball with concomitant growth, popularity, and profits. Thanks to urbanization stemming from the Industrial Revolution and the explosion of media, baseball entered a Golden Age as the National Pastime.

It was against this backdrop that a group of investors conceived a plan to establish a third major league to rival the National and American Leagues. It was called the Federal League. Their plan was simple – the Federal League would gain legitimacy by hiring the best talent away from the established league by offering higher salaries and other incentives. In 1913, the Federal League operated franchises in six cities in direct competition with major league baseball. The next season promised even greater competition.

The city of Baltimore was all abuzz because the Federal League had announced the establishment of a team there for the 1914 season. They would be called the Baltimore Terrapins and play in a brand new ballpark on 29th Street and Greenmount Avenue directly across the street from the minor league Baltimore Orioles of the soon-to-be-renamed International League.

In January, the excitement reached a fever pitch when the team announced that it had signed Oscar Gnarltz to a three-year contract as player-manager. Gnarltz had been a stellar performer for the Nationals in the nearby Washington market. He would be instrumental in recruiting the top players from the Washington and Philadelphia teams. Not since the 1903 season when the American League had moved the Baltimore franchise to New York City where they played as the Highlanders, had the city of Baltimore been home to a major league baseball team. Many Baltimoreans looked forward to having a major league team in their community again.

The elder George Ruth was one of those people. He calculated the Terrapins would benefit his saloon business, especially on game days when beer-drinking fans would crowd the neighborhood bars. There was another reason George senior was excited about the prospects of the Terrapins in his city – he had heard that his son was one of the top sandlot players in Baltimore. On a wintry evening, shortly after the announcement by the Terrapins that they had just signed Oscar Gnarltz to run the Baltimore franchise, George sat at a table across from the bar and composed a letter to the new manager.

In the letter, George set forth the pitching achievements of his son and requested a tryout. He was a southpaw who routinely recorded double-digit strikeouts against much older competition. George was not a man of letters; he had barely finished grammar school. His hands sweated as he fashioned a letter to Mr. Gnarltz. It took nine drafts before he produced a legible and coherent copy. He hand delivered the letter to the offices of the Terps. And then he waited. Little did he know that thousands of fathers across the

# FEBRUARY 1914 ST. MARY'S LAKE, BALTIMORE, MARYLAND

country had sent similar letters to the Terrapins applying for positions with the new, major league franchise.

Gnarltz's reply was remarkably candid, or brutally blunt, depending on the point of view of the reader. Either way, it left no reason for hope. The Terps were only interested in players with major league pedigrees and had zero interest in amateurs from the Baltimore sandlots. Gnarltz's poor judgment would be compounded by his vile actions in the World Series five years later.

"It's freezing out. Where are you headed, Jidgie?" asked Fats.

The rangy teenager had a big grin on his face. He pointed to the ice skates that were tied together and slung over his shoulder. Two years had passed since his mother's passing, he had just celebrated his nineteenth birthday and it was a beautiful, crisp morning. It was too wonderful a day to stay cooped up inside.

"Me and a bunch of the guys are going over to the lake to slice some ice. Wanna come?" he laughed.

"OK, but don't get into trouble. I know some of those boys don't give a crap about anything. So don't get sucked into stuff that will get you suspended from baseball."

"Hey, don't sweat it. I know what I'm doing."

"Yeah, yeah. Have fun. I'll meet you there later after I finish studying," Fats chuckled.

Fats knew that his friend had the body of a man, but the playfulness of a kid. Jidgie did not have a mean bone in his body; but sometimes, well, sometimes he could get a little carried away. Just last month, Brother Matthias had to apologize to Mrs. Galetti because Jidgie decided to use her son Bruno as a human bowling ball that Jidgie hurled over the ice toward some other kids that he had arranged like bowling pins. When Agnes Schultz described the incident to Brother Matthias she could hardly finish the story because she was laughing so hard. Through breathless gasps and teary guffaws she recreated a comical scene of Jidgie folding Bruno into a ball and then grabbing him by the belt on his coat and flinging him along the frozen surface. Bruno was giggling hilariously as he spun with deadly accuracy toward the boy pins. Bruno hit Teddy Schmidt and Henry Gunther with such force that they smashed into the rest of the bunch, cutting them down at the feet. Except for Ray Jones who kept his balance, all the boy pins collapsed. That is until Bruno bounced off Gunny and went airborne. He flew toward Ray who wind-milled his arms to avoid him. Bruno hit Ray with such velocity that Ray could not hold him. Ray wobbled and then fell backwards while Jidgie yelled, "Timmberrr! A strike!" at the top of his lungs.

With his best friend gone, the dorm was preternaturally quiet. Jidgie's constant chatter and high energy kept the dorm hopping. Fats couldn't study, it was too quiet. He bundled up and trudged off to the lake. It did not take long for him to get into the swing of things.

"Hey, Jidgie, come over here," yelled Fats. "We're starting a chain and we need you to run the edge. No one skates as fast as you. Come on!"

With Fats at one end of a line and Jidgie at the other end, the skaters pushed off. It did not take long for the skaters on the outer edge to propel themselves at top speed to keep up. On the second lap two skaters inside of Jidgie fell off, unable to keep the pace. Rather than falling off with them, Jidgie pumped his legs faster and caught up with the next innermost skater. Left with only the fastest skaters, the line whipped around the lake in a dizzying circle.

"There he is, Jack, the tall boy at the end. That's your boy. He's quite an athlete," said Brother Matthias pointing toward the whirling skaters.

The three men descended toward the lake and approached the whip line. Matthias put his fingers to his lips and unleashed a shrill whistle. Jidgie looked toward the brother and waved, never breaking stride. Matthias signaled for the boy to join them. Jidgie's response was to release hands with the inner skater and accelerate. He was traveling at breakneck speed toward the men when he realized that one of the younger inmates was wobbling on skates into his path. With the balletic grace of Nijinsky, Jidgie launched himself into the air. For a moment it appeared that he would not clear the youngster. However, Jidgie lifted his legs to his stomach and passed over the boy easily.

Jidgie landed with shock-absorber legs and shifted his weight to catch the blades of his skates in a stopping maneuver. A shower of shaved ice exuded from his blades as he halted before the Brother and his guests. Matthias and the others stood with their front-sides coated with ice flakes. Jidgie smiled and bowed from the waist. When he stood upright, he was grinning from ear-to-ear.

"George, I'd like you to meet Mr. John Dunn. He is the owner and manager of the Baltimore Orioles, a professional baseball team in the International League. And this is his associate, Mr. Fritz Maisel, third baseman for the New York Yankees."

The grin disappeared and Jidgie doffed his cap, "It's a pleasure to meet you both."

Jidgie and all the boys knew of Jack Dunn by reputation – he was the embodiment of the means to achieving the elusive goal of playing professional baseball. Yet, for poor boys living in an institution, Dunn seemed more like a mythical creature than an actual person.

Jack Dunn was a baseball lifer. He began his major league career with the Brooklyn Bridesmaids and ended it as a middle infielder for the New York Giants. After his playing career ended he became a successful manager and then franchise owner. At five foot-nine, he was taller than most. With his pale complexion, pug nose, and intense blue eyes, Jidgie thought that he could be mistaken for a giant, oversized leprechaun.

The affable Irishman had experienced success, leading his teams to pennants for more than a decade. Now, in his early forties, Dunn was facing the challenge of his baseball life. His beloved Baltimore Orioles were confronted by extreme competition in his home market of Baltimore from the Baltimore Terrapins of the newly-formed Federal League. The off-season scuttlebutt was that the Terps were loaded with renegade major leaguers who jumped to the new league for exorbitant sums of money. The only way for Dunn to remain competitive was to find cheap, young talent.

He had been tipped off about the Ruth kid by Joe Engel, a journeyman pitcher with the Washington Nationals. It seemed that Joe had gone to Baltimore to pitch an exhibition game for his alma mater against St. Mary's the previous fall. While waiting for his game, Joe watched a young, gangly southpaw strike out eighteen or twenty in a preliminary game. The southpaw from the industrial school outpitched a young right-hander named Bill Morrisette, a college pitcher who was generally regarded as the best prospect in Maryland. Engel was so impressed with the young lefty's natural talent that he mentioned it to Jack Dunn when he ran into him on the train back to Washington. Dunn put the information in his mental vault.

Jack Dunn ate, drank, and slept baseball. Winter was the worst time of the year. He liked to quote Rogers Hornsby who said, "People ask me what I do in the winter when there is no baseball, I'll tell you what I do. I stare out the window and wait for spring."

So, it was no surprise that during the doldrums of February, he asked his buddy Fritz Maisel to accompany him on a scouting jaunt out at St. Mary's. Fritz also had cabin fever and agreed. He had played for Dunn's Orioles the previous season until Dunn sold his contract to the Yankees. The diminutive Maisel was nicknamed "Flash," for his base stealing ability. Like his pal Dunn, he was an astute talent evaluator. Jidgie was in awe to be in the presence of a real, live major leaguer. Wow, if Colina could see him now.

"Do you like to skate?" asked Dunn.

# FEBRUARY 1914 ST. MARY'S LAKE, BALTIMORE, MARYLAND

"It's fun to go fast," said Jidgie.

"George likes to do everything fast, Jack. He especially likes to throw the horsehide fast," said Matthias. Jidgie looked down at his feet and grinned.

"You know, I used to dabble as a pitcher myself. I could give you some pointers if you'd like. Let's go down by the field and have us a catch, OK?"

Jidgie looked to Matthias who nodded. The men and the boy walked over to a clearing across from the school. Magically, a ball appeared from Dunn's pocket. He flipped to Jidgie, who wristed back a throw. As they settled into to the rhythm of playing catch, they widened the distance until they had drifted about sixty feet apart. Dunn removed his winter glove from his throwing hand. Jidgie had no gloves and just caught Dunn's throws with his bare hands. Jidgie was delighted to be playing catch after many weeks without baseball due to the snowy winter. He removed his jacket and wheeled in a few zingers that stung Jack's hand through the thin leather glove. His trained eye appreciated the natural fluidity of George's throwing motion. He admired the boy's trim, muscular physique.

"Show me your best pitches," said Dunn, lowering himself into a crouch with his left hand held waist high.

Attracted by the popping of the baseball on leather, a small crowd of inmates had gathered around the pair. Pretty soon, there was a buzz of excitement punctuated by cheers and exhortations. Dunn maintained a serious expression as he coaxed the pitcher to hit the target as Jack moved it around the strike zone. Internally, Dunn was almost overwhelmed with excitement from George's raw talent and the bone-numbing pain in his catching hand.

Although Jidgie was throwing effortlessly, the ball was thumping into Dunn's hand with ferocious speed and movement. It was the movement of the pitches that impressed Dunn the most. It also caused the most pain because the late, unpredictable darting action prevented Dunn from catching the ball with the meaty part of his hand. Instead the ball was driving into his joints and the bony areas in the crannies of his hands.

"Hey, Flash, why don't you stand in the batter's box while George here pitches?"

Maisel took his stance next to the plate that Dunn had drawn in the snow. Flash nodded to Dunnie in appreciation as George pumped in strike after strike, hitting the target with deadly accuracy. At Dunn's suggestion, Maisel switched sides and affected a left-handed batting stance.

The session ended abruptly when Dunn called for a curve and Jidgie let fly with a breaker whose seams sizzled as it approached the imaginary dish. The ball headed straight for Flash's head. Unaccustomed to batting from that side of the plate, Flash panicked and spun into a heap on the ground in a herky-jerky motion. Just before the ball reached the plate, it dived at an impossible angle, so quickly and sharply that it fooled Dunn's reflexes. There was a nasty thump as the baseball careened off Dunn's shin. He tried to stifle a yelp of pain as he hopped around on one leg to relieve the hurt.

The boys assembled on the edge of the action roared their approval. They laughed and pointed as the two professional ballplayers recovered from the embarrassment and hurt. Between guffaws, Fats commented to Jonas, "That's sure gonna leave a mark!"

Brother Matthias rushed to Dunn's side and supported the hopping man. Matthias started to apologize, but was interrupted.

"It was all my fault. I never expected the bloody, excuse me Brother, the darn thing to break that much, that quickly. Brother, let's go to your office and sign this boy up. He definitely has the talent to go far in this game."

"Ok, but you have not seen him hit. He really can maul the ball."

"I trust your opinion. If he can hit half as good as he can twirl, then he's going to be the snake's hips."

The three men plus Jidgie crowded into the office of Brother Matthias. Standing against the back bookcase, a trickle of perspiration rolled down Jidgie's back. He was excited and overwhelmed by what was happening. Feeling like a spare piece of furniture, Jidgie stood off to the side listening. Thank goodness Brother Matthias was there looking out for him.

The Xaverian towered over the two smaller ballplayers. Matthias knew that the professionals were impressed with Jidgie. He felt the weight of responsibility as the boy's legal guardian. Negotiating contracts was not something taught in seminary. Matthias prayed silently for wisdom.

Once Brother Matthias had treated the men to some hot tea, the negotiation began. After the preliminaries had been discussed, Dunn spoke.

"George, that was some display you gave out there in the snow. I can hardly imagine how you would do in a green pasture on a warm, summer day. We want you to join our Baltimore ball club," said Dunn. The boy glanced at Matthias who nodded.

"That sounds swell, sir, except I don't have much money to pay to join. I only get twenty cents per shirt, but I'll work hard to get it for you."

The men chuckled.

"That won't be necessary, George. The way it works is that we will pay you to come play. We can give you six hundred dollars for the season. How about it?"

Jidgie, his eyebrows twisted in a questioning pose, again looked to Matthias.

"Yes, George, Mr. Dunn here will pay you that sum. Playing ball will be your job. You will be expected to be at the ball yard on time and do whatever Mr. Dunn asks you to do for the team," said the brother.

"OK," said the young man with hesitation in his voice, his

shoulders slumped. "May I be excused?"

"Sure, in the meantime, I will finalize some points with Mr. Dunn."

Jidgie nodded and walked out of the room. Matthias thought he heard the faint sound of retching through the closed door.

Dunn gave Matthias a broad grin as he pumped the big man's hand.

"Don't worry, Brother, I'll treat him like he's my own babe. You will be proud of him. I promise."

Matthias crossed himself and gestured skyward as if to say God will be watching you.

Matthias had mixed feelings. While he trusted that Dunn meant to care for George, the brother knew that his charge would be subjected to all sorts of temptations. Without the close supervision of the Xaverians, how would he react? Matthias felt the emotions that every father experienced when one of his children left the nest. Of course, that did not make it any easier.

The brother walked to the dormitory building looking for George. However, he was surprised to find it empty. Matthias walked over to George's bed and perused the nightstand next to it. He picked up George's hymnal and flipped open the cover. He smiled at the inscription he found there.

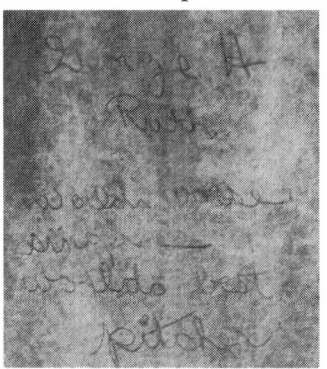

(courtesy of the Babe Ruth Birthplace Museum)

*George H.*

*Ruth*

*Worlds worst singer --*

*Worlds best pitcher*

# FEBRUARY 1914 ST. MARY'S LAKE, BALTIMORE, MARYLAND

Where was George, he wondered? After questioning several loitering students to no avail, Matthias had an idea. He strode purposefully to a building across the campus and up the stairs until he came to a long, narrow room with a high ceiling. Dust motes illuminated by the fading afternoon sun filled the Tailor Shop. Arrayed across the length were a series of sewing stations, each with a shirt block, fabric layout area and a sewing machine. George sat in the far corner where the advanced tailors worked. He was sitting at his sewing machine, not moving. Normally, George was a frenetic blur of motion. To see him still was like watching a baby sleep; his features and body could be observed without the distraction of motion. Matthias paused, just looking. He thought that he was doing the right thing. Lord, please watch over him.

"George," he said, clearing his throat, "I expected to find you in the dorm. What are you doing here?"

"Just thinking, you know," said George, his tone subdued. When he turned his face up, his eyes were red.

"It'll be fine, George. You'll see. It'll be a grand adventure."

"I don't know, brother. I've been thinking that this is my home and the fellas here are my family. I can't abandon them. The varsity needs me. We're favored to take the league this year."

"That's not what really matters. There comes a time to move on, a time to leave behind childish ways. You are always welcome to return. We'll all be here."

"That's what I mean. You'll all be here and I'll be gone," said George shaking his head and suppressing a tear. Matthias sat next to him and put his arm around the boy. They were silent for several minutes.

"I can't go. Boss, I got a girl waiting for me back in New York. She's expecting me to work there like I do every summer."

"George, you should talk to her. I'm sure that she would not want to stand in your way. You've always dreamed of playing professional baseball. You even said so in your hymnal. It's what you excel at."

Jidgie smiled in a self-congratulatory manner. Was the Boss right about Colina? What if he lost Colina and then he failed with Mr. Dunn? Then, he would have nothing.

"Anyway, it don't matter because you have the paper. The paper says I can't go. That's what you always told me. The paper won't let me go."

This statement perplexed Matthias, until he realized what the boy meant.

"Well, George, in a way you are correct. The legal guardian paper provides that we have the right to care for you and to make decisions on your behalf until you are an adult. It also gives us the right to delegate your care to qualified caregivers. In other words, if we think that someone like Mr. Dunn can watch over you like a guardian angel, then, we can let him. Of course, we would never do anything that would harm you."

He let that sink in. Then, he said, "George, remember when we studied President Roosevelt in history class?" The boy nodded.

"Remember the President's speech about the Man in the Arena? Roosevelt believed that we should not stand on the sidelines and watch others in the action. We should jump into the action with both feet and do our best. You have a special gift, George. President Roosevelt would urge you to jump into the action. This opportunity may be your gateway."

Jidgie set his lips. His eyes steeled toward a purpose. However, doubt was also present. Matthias searched for the perfect doubt-remover. Then, a quote came to mind. He smiled.

"George, what is President Roosevelt's most famous quote?"

The boy shrugged, dully.

"Here it is and it is perfect for this situation." He paused. Then, he delivered the quote, followed by a hearty laugh.

"'Speak softly and carry a big stick; you will go far.'[ix] There it is, George. That should be your motto."

# February 1914 St. Mary's Lake, Baltimore, Maryland

Matthias sensed that George was still not convinced. Perhaps, what was needed was a meal and a good night's sleep. That seemed to be the answer to many of life's dilemmas.

"George, you and I have spoken about how God has a plan for each of us. It was his plan that I would be there when you needed me. We can never know in advance what His plan is until after it unfolds. I think that you and I should pray tonight and ask God to show us whether this is His plan for you. What do you say? Let's go to the dining hall now. You and I can talk again in the morning, OK?"

A sigh of relief escaped Jidgie's lips.

● ● ●

Meanwhile, outside of a city over forty-six hundred miles away, another nineteen-year old student was in a snowy forest. His name was Gavrilo. An older man exhorted him to hit the target. Like Jidgie, the youngster demonstrated uncanny accuracy, striking the target time after time. Gavrilo's target was not a baseball mitt; it was a silhouette of a man which hung from a tree. Bullets from Gavrilo's pistol struck the heart of the target.

"Excellent, my young friend," said Dragutin, leader of the Black Hand, a secret organization within the Serbian Army. "You are ready to change the course of history!"

The boy smiled at the praise, but wondered in his heart whether he could pull the trigger when the time came. He shared his doubts with no one.

To Be Continued

# Bonus

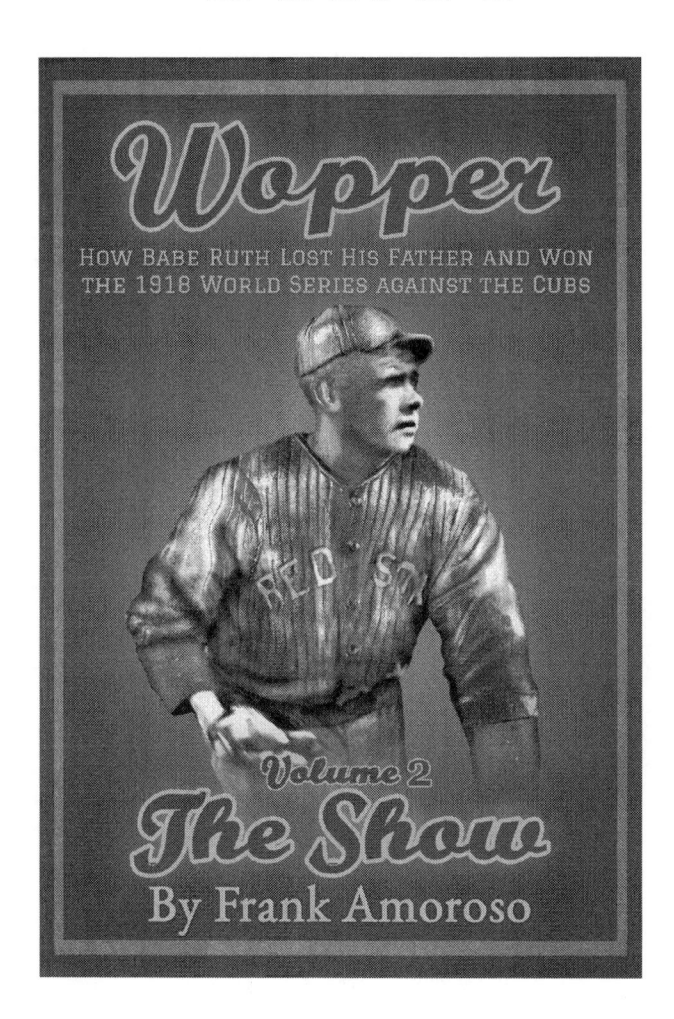

## Wopper

How Babe Ruth Lost His Father and Won the 1918 World Series against the Cubs

### Volume 2
### The Show

By Frank Amoroso

St. Mary's Industrial School Baseball Team. Babe Ruth back row center (circa 1913)

# 1

# February, 1914
# Baltimore, Maryland &
# Fayetteville, North Carolina

*Two roads diverged in a wood, and I—
I took the one less traveled by,
And that has made all the difference.
~ Robert Frost, The Road Not Taken*

Groggy, he picked up his pillow for the umpteenth time. He rammed the edge of the pillow between his ear and elbow and creased the remainder over his other ear. His feet protruded from beneath the sheets, hanging over the edge of the bed. His plans, to the extent that he had thought them through, did not include going to Fayetteville to become a professional ballplayer. No, he had a vague, hazy idea that, even under the most generous definition of plan, could not be termed a plan. Simply put, Jidgie figured that he would get a job in the Garment District in New York City and hang out with Colina. To him, it made perfect sense. Jack Dunn had just thrown a baseball-bat sized monkey wrench into his future.

Jidgie wondered whether Colina would want to go with him to Fayetteville, even though he was sure that she had no idea where Fayetteville was located. On the other hand, maybe he would be an abysmal failure and get cut by the Orioles. In that case, he could head north to the City. What did the Boss always say – Nothing ventured, nothing gained? No, no, he would not fail. He was the best player around, it was not even close. Jidgie knew that he was destined to succeed.

Brother Matthias seemed to want him to go with Mr. Dunn. The ease with which he dismissed the importance of the custody paper left Jidgie with an uneasy feeling. He thought that the paper meant that the Xaverians were his parents. Since his mother was gone, the brothers were in a legal sense his father. Or, were they? What would his father say? Would he even care? OK, he reached a sleep-infused decision. He would go talk to Big George about it. With that procrastinating approach resolved, he lapsed into a deep sleep.

When the mail was delivered that day, George's hopes were raised when he received an envelope bearing the bright, new logo of the Baltimore Terrapins. It must be a response from Gnarltz to his letter. He was encouraged by the heft of the envelope. Maybe it included a contract. Tearing open the letter the first thing he encountered was a flyer promoting the sale of season's tickets for the major league Terrapins. Tucked behind the flyer was an artist's rendering of the new ballpark. Terrapin Park was under construction along 29th Street, stretching through to 30th, east of

Vineyard Lane and the 2900 block of Guilford Ave.

Hidden under the promotional material was another missive. Like rejection letters since the dawn of letters, Gnarltz' response was succinct and definitive. Thank you for you inquiry. We regret to inform you that we have no need of your services. Since our objective is to build our fan base, we are only seeking candidates with major league experience and demonstrated accomplishments in professional baseball. The letter ended with the obligatory best of luck in your future endeavors. George hung his head in disappointment. He had convinced himself that his son would use baseball to lift himself out of Pigtown. The bartender had suffered too much disappointment in his life to hope that the closing of one door might lead to the opening of another.

The following day, Jidgie boarded the trolley on his way to visit his father. He arrived after lunch to take advantage of the saloon's slowest time. When George saw his son get off the trolley he removed the Gnarltz letter from the counter. No need to share the bad news with the boy.

"Hey, Pop."

"Hi, Jidge, what are you doing here? Need money?" he said with not a small dose of sarcasm.

"Naw, I wanted to tell you about a meeting I had yesterday."

"Who'd you meet with?"

"Do you know who John Dunn is?"

"Do you mean Jack Dunn, the Orioles' magnate?"

"Yeah, that's him. Well, yesterday he offered me a job."

"As what, the team janitor?"

Jidgie paused, second-guessing his decision to come to see his father.

"Will you just stop it for once? I'm trying to get your advice and all you want to do is belittle me," said the son, his voice rising in spite of every effort to control it. He tried to remember one serious discussion that they had ever had. The only one he could recall happened when his father talked about the travails his mother had suffered during the course of their marriage. Jidgie learned things that he had never known about his parents. The friction caused by the multiple deaths of their infants had savaged their marriage. Perhaps, the treatment of the boy and his rebellious reaction was a manifestation of the family sorrows.

"Son, you gotta live your own life. Whatever choice you make is the right one. Just realize that once you make it, there is no going back."

Back at St. Mary's, Matthias went about business as usual. He figured that it was the type of decision that George alone had to reach. To avoid undue influence from his fellow inmates, Matthias suggested that George stay with his father. For his part, Jidgie struggled with how to get to know Colina's feelings. He lacked the time and money to go to the City. He wished that there was a speedy, convenient way to discuss it with her. Neither had access to a telephone that would assure them the needed privacy. He concluded that the best way was to use the method that had sufficed through the ages. He would reveal his dilemma in a letter. This decision had the same, predictable results – it was slow, letters crossed in the mail and actual communication was thwarted.

Spring training was scheduled to begin in March. Jack Dunn told Brother Matthias that the team was leaving from the Keenan Hotel on March 2nd. The brother said that he would tell the boy, but, that the young man had yet not decided whether he would be on the train. Dunn was about to fly off the handle when Matthias told him to give George time to reach the most important decision of his young life.

"Why don't you just tell him to get his butt on that train? You know he'll never have another opportunity like this."

"That may be what you think, but he's got to reach that conclusion on his own."

"Right. After Monday, if he's not on that train, no deal," said Dunn, his eyes nearly bugging out of his head. He left the brother's office muttering to himself and shaking his head.

Meanwhile, back at Ruth's Saloon, Jidgie stared out the window searching for the letter carrier. It was almost two weeks since he had sent a letter to Colina explaining his options and requesting her guidance. Actually, he was desperate for her to tell him to come to New York to be with her. As fate would have it, on the day the letter was delivered, Colina's father had thrown the day's mail onto the kitchen table. Jidgie's letter was on top and had slid off the table and had fallen behind the radiator. No one noticed.

On the Sunday before the drop dead date, a frantic Jidgie went to St. Mary's to use the phone to call Rosina's Restaurant in a last-ditch effort to reach Colina. High winds and heavy snow battered the trolley over the entire four mile trip. The worst winter storm in his lifetime had already dumped almost a foot of snow. There was no sign of a let-up.

The wind nearly yanked the door out of Brother Mathias' hand when he let George in. The grounds were covered white. Snow had drifted along the outfield fences to cover all evidence that a ball field existed there. Matthias listened to George's plea and ushered him into his office. He dialed the phone number that George gave him and handed over the receiver. Jidgie pressed the device against his ear so hard that Matthias saw a white circle develop on the boy's skin. With a look of intense concentration, his lower lip lost under his upper teeth, Jidgie listened as the circuits crackled through the connections up the coast to the City. The next thing he heard was voice of an operator.

"I'm sorry, sir, we are experiencing a severe winter storm, lines are down in New Jersey. We are unable to complete the connection. Try back tomorrow."

The phone went dead.

"Tomorrow will be too late!" he screamed at the phone.

A bear with its leg caught in sharp teeth of a bear-trap could not have had wilder eyes than Jidgie. His conflicting emotions were tearing him apart.

"It's your fault. You can't just sign me over to Dunn like I'm a piece of meat. I should have another year before I have to decide," shouted Jidgie, who bolted for the door. A stunned Matthias thought he heard George mutter under his breath something that sounded like '. . . just like my Pops.'

The retreating young man probably did not hear Brother Matthias say, "*Noli timere,* Don't be afraid. George, you'll make it."

Another night where sleep evaded him. He had lost count. All he knew was that his pillow felt like a stone, providing no comfort. Attempts to shift his position yielded no relief for the dull headache that had taken up residence in this skull. He knew that until he made his decision the headache and sleeplessness would persist. He thought, maybe the armchair in the living room might be comfortable enough to induce sleep. Naw, he had tried it a few hours ago and the smell of his father's tobacco and the ever-so-faint aroma of his mother's perfume that Mamie wore when she was feeling blue, robbed him of slumber. A clock ticked in the kitchen, he heard the wind slipping through the alley like a burglar escaping. The shutters creaked.

He roamed the apartment quietly, slowly. From the kitchen window he saw dim illumination. It came from the direction of the railyards. There were men working the night shift throughout the city – in the relentless darkness mechanics, bakers, brewers, and teamsters kept the metropolis machine repaired and prepared for the next day. Bored and anxious he decided to take a walk in the darkness. No destination, just something to do.

Wandering the streets aimlessly in concentric circles, he drifted toward the railyards. Subconsciously, he knew that the yards would facilitate his fate. Within the next day or so he would board a train – whether it would take him north to New York and Colina or south to Fayetteville and Jack Dunn was the question.

Before long he was at Bailey's Wye. The wind buffeted him as he trudged toward the roundhouse. He pulled his cap down tight and lifted his collar in a vain effort to stay warm. Steam, light, and noise emerged from the roundhouse. He could hear the shouts of men at work at the turntable. Drawing closer he saw a crew attaching a large wedge-shaped plow to the front of a locomotive.

The foreman of the crew saw Jidgie eyeing the operation and approached him.

"We could use an extra hand to steady the plow while the mechanics attach it to the front of that there jack," he said gesturing toward the plow that appeared like a stallion trussed for branding.

"Sure, I'll pitch in. What do I have to do?"

"Go over with Tom and the boys and help them with that block and tackle to raise or lower the plow when needed."

Jidgie welcomed the physical exertion which distracted his mind.

Later when the operation was done, Jidgie learned that another jack would be attached to the first engine to form a doubleheader. The railroad term doubled as a baseball term and made Jidgie smile. Thus equipped, the train would make its way north through the snow-blocked tracks to New York. Jidgie wondered whether he would be on that train.

All through the night and next day he vacillated over which direction to travel. North to Colina? Or, south to the Orioles?

Learn what happens next in

## *Wopper*

How Babe Ruth Lost His Father and
Won the 1918 World Series Against the Cubs

## *Volume 2 The Show*

# GLOSSARY OF EARLY 20TH CENTURY IDIOMS AND BASEBALL SLANG

**Agate**, n. – baseball; apple; horsehide; the pill

**Aggregation**, n. - team

**Annie Oakley**, n. – base on balls

**Bingle**, n. – a well-struck hit, a single

**Bop in the beezer**, v. – punch someone in the nose

**Box artist**, n. – pitcher; ball tosser; or twirler

**Bush, bushes**, n. – lower level baseball, minor leagues

**Busher**, n. – term of scorn for a low class player, prone to rinky-dink or unprofessional actions

**Butterfinger**, v. – error, fielding muff, as in Max Flack admitting that, "I butterfingered the play and am unanimously elected as the goat."

**Cake**, n. - dandy or vain ball player who obsesses over his personal appearance to the detriment of his game

**Candy kid**, n. – swatter who drives in a run

**Circuit drive**, n. – home run

**Coachers**, n. – base coaches

**Cudgel**, n. – baseball bat

**Emery ball**, n. – when the pitcher scuffs a ball with sandpaper or an emery board to cause the ball to move erratically

**Fade**, n. – screwball, pitch that moves away from the batter, perfected by Christy Matthewson

**Fans**, n. – cranks; bugs

**Flivver**, n. – small car with a rough ride

**Frank**, n. – walk, ball on balls

**Fumble**, v. – to commit a fielding error

**Get his alley**, v. – find weak spot in a batter's swing

# GLOSSARY

**Get your nanny**, v. – be irritated, as in "Don't let him get your nanny." Derived from nanny goat.

**Horse collar**, n. – when batter goes hitless, he wears a horse collar.

**Horse-hide**, n. – name for baseball based on the leather covering used

**Hoodoo**, n., v. – jinx, superstition that player or object has unnatural mastery

**Hot stove, hot stove league**, n. – off-season when fans gather around hot stove to discuss baseball and potential personnel changes

**Jape**, - a practical joke, a jest

**Jinegar**, n. - term for pep or spirit

**Jounce**, v. – to jolt or bounce, as in, he jounced a hit through the infield

**Kalsomine**, n., - whitewash, shut out, as in, he put the kalsomine on the Cubs

**Knuckle party**, n. – fight, fisticuffs

**Lamps**, n. – a player's eyes

**Leather**, n. – baseball glove or defensive ability, as in, he's good with the leather; or, he can really flash the leather

**Lemonball**, n. –leather baseball handstitched with two circumferential rows of stitches

**Magnate**, n. – owner of a baseball club

**Mauler**, n. – power hitter

**Necktie party**, n. – a hanging bee, lynching

**Outfield**, n. – garden

**Outfielder**, n. – gardener; garden tender

**Piffle**, n. – nonsense, as in "Don't hand me that piffle."

**Pinch**, n. – a difficult or pivotal part of a game

**Pink slip**, n. – refers to the action of a manager removing a pitcher from the game, as in, with a disgusted grunt, Huggins gave Thomas the pink slip and signaled for a reliever from the bullpen.

**Platter**, n. – home plate, as in, he crossed the platter for a tally

**Policeman of the diamond** – umpire

**Shineball, shiner**, n. – when the pitcher rubs a ball vigorously to create a shiny area to cause the ball to move erratically

**Slab**, n. – the mound; rubber

**Slabman**, n. – pitcher, boxman

**Slants**, n. – pitches

**Snake's hips**, adj. – something excellent

**Snuggle-pupping**, v. – making out, passionate kissing

**Southpaw**, n. – left-handed thrower

**Stepping in the bucket**, v. – when the lead foot of the batter pulls away from the plate

**Striker**, n. – batter; swatter

**Throng**, n. – large crowd of fans or bugs

**Trolley-wire**, v. – to strike a baseball with such force that its trajectory appears as straight and true as the wire that provides electricity to a trolley car

**Wagon tongue**, n. – baseball bat

**Whiff**, n – a strikeout, often by virtue of a swing and miss

**Willow**, n. – baseball bat

**Yannigan**, n. – a rookie, a player not on the regular team

**Zeppelin**, v. – To hit the ball high and long; *esp.* to hit a home run. Now apparently *disused*

**Zipper**, n. – fastball

# End Notes

i Wooden, John with Jamison, Steve, *Wooden: A Lifetime of Observations and Reflections On and Off the Court*, McGraw-Hill Education, New York (1997) p. 5.

ii Brother Gilbert, C.F. X., *Young Babe Ruth*, McFarland & Company, Inc., Jefferson, North Carolina (1999) p. 11.

iii Ruth, George Herman "Babe," *"Started Swat Career Early,"* Boston Post, August 9, 1920, p. 7, col. 1.

iv Ruth, George Herman "Babe," "The Kids Can't Take It If We Don't Give It!" Guideposts (October, 1948).

v Everett, Marshall, "Lest We Forget" Chicago's Awful Theater Horror, Memorial Publishing, Inc. (1904) p. 365.

vi Fitzpatrick, Vincent, *H.L. Menchen*, p. 6, Mercer University Press, Macon Georgia, (2004).

vii Leisman, Louis, "Fats," "I Was with BABE RUTH at St. Mary's" Aberdeen, Maryland, (1956) p. 15.

viii Deposition by George H. Ruth, *George H. Ruth vs. Katie Ruth*, Baltimore Circuit Court No. 8962B p. 7 – 8.

ix Letter from then-New York Governor Theodore Roosevelt to Harry Sprague, January 26, 1900, quoting West African proverb. https://www.loc.gov/exhibits/treasures/trm139.html

# Acknowledgements

The creation of a work of historical fiction requires assistance from many people and sources. *Wopper* is no exception. Without the amazing capabilities of the Internet, this series would have taken much more time to research and write. Similarly, without the generosity of Babe Ruth scholars this series would not have been possible. Mike Gibbons, executive director of the Babe Ruth Birthplace Museum, was exceptionally supportive and generous with his time and materials. Fred Shoken and Bill Jenkinson provided excellent information and leads to fascinating Babe Ruth sources.

I was blessed to have the insight and editorial suggestions of several talented people. I am most grateful to Dr. Robert Kuncio-Raleigh and Shaun Cherewich for their dedication and insightful edits. Larry Keith, former neighbor and top executive at *Sports Illustrated* provided a unique perspective and wealth of experience that greatly improved the final manuscript.

The biography project of the talented members of SABR (Society for American Baseball Research) was a constant source of anecdotal and background information that helped to provide depth and authenticity to this work. I am proud to be a member of this august organization.

Last, but not least, I wish to thank my family for their never-ending support and guidance. My children Valerie, Jenna, Jason and Louis inspire me. Words cannot suffice to express my love and gratitude to my wife, Rhonda for everything she does to make me a better writer and person.

Made in the USA
Charleston, SC
04 February 2017